WORMWOOD

WORMWOOD

BY D.J. LEVIEN

MIRAMAX
B O O K S
HYPERION
N E W   Y O R K

Copyright © 1999 D.J. Levien

Design by Robin Arzt

Library of Congress Cataloging-in-Publication Data

Levien, David.
    Wormwood / by D.J. Levien. — 1st ed.
        p.   cm.
    "Miramax books."
    ISBN: 0-7868-6506-7
    I. Title.
    PS3562.E8887W67   1999
    813'.54—dc21   98-43840
                                                                        CIP

FIRST EDITION

10 9 8 7 6 5 4 3 2 1

For Melissa,
who led me out of the darkness

CHAPTER ONE

The town where the laughing images were made would always be Wormwood to me. It was where I had lived for the past two years, but it was not my home. The place ran on lies, fear, and fresh meat, and drinking absinthe in underground clubs had become all the rage that summer. I was still in the liquor's grip as I moved slowly toward work, trapped in the freeway's tight snake of traffic. Hordes of young men and women crept along around me in their shiny leased cars, filled with nagging disquiet or gripped outright by the fear in their guts. A man to my left leaned forward in his seat and dragged anxiously on a cigarette, his vehicle the only place he was still permitted to smoke. A woman to my right looked not at the road but into her rearview mirror as she smeared inky mascara onto her lashes. I could sense their uneasiness. I knew it was almost over for me too. We were bound for the same or similar destinations—the movie studios—strange, be-

hemoth places built by and for the incredible flickering celluloid entertainments we all had a hand in creating. We
stopped and started in the early morning glare, checking our
watches nervously, pulling up too close to the bumper in front
of us, only to lurch hard on our brakes again and again. All
of us, whether wealthy or desperate to become so, naturally
beautiful or slovenly and in need of surgical enhancement,
talented or chronically uninspired, had one thing in common:
we wanted. We wanted to get in, we wanted to make movies,
we wanted to profit by this, to be made special from it, but
above all we just wanted to remain. It wasn't easy, and those
around me knew well the very real possibility of being swept
into oblivion at any moment. Panic united with our closely
monitored emissions, and poured forth from our cars. The
brown hills along the roadside were choked with ugly dry
brush that quivered visibly in response.

I made my way amongst them, jockeying my old car from
one congested lane to another as if in an extremely slow race.
I wondered what it would be like to walk to work, and how I
even managed to show up every morning. How I toiled my day
out of days, a slave to the grind, a hero only in my nonexistent
sleep. At last I reached my off-ramp, made my turn, and
passed through the great studio gates. The fictional cities and
worlds of the back lot, the humpbacked roofs of the sound
stages, rose before me in the distance. Tame squirrels chat-
tered in the already potent morning heat, and I lurched on my
brakes again, this time for several grown men wearing saddle
shoes who rode in front of me on brightly painted bicycles as
if this were the most natural thing in the world for grown men

to do. I parked my car and entered the great modern building of glass and pale umber stone, known as "The Bunker," which housed my office.

Eye-level towers of screenplays rose from the faux wood grain of my desk, and as I sat down, the stacks of printed material obscured view of me from the outside world, and my view of it. Each script was a well-intentioned paper larva, a painstaking creation by an individual author. Each represented one person's dream, but for me each was another stone in the wall behind which I spent my days. Unable to bring myself to read one, I instead spread the trade papers in front of me and began poring over the repetitive stories of blood and glory that filled them each day. I sipped my morning coffee with regret for how it washed away the faint traces of licorice flavor remaining in my mouth from last night's drinking.

How had absinthe, the fabled emerald green liqueur, become the latest fad in this town of fads? It did have a pleasant flavor and a devastatingly high alcohol content. But mere alcoholism was out of fashion, so it was more than that. The drink had been famous amongst many of the great artists of history, and that gave it cachet. Van Gogh, Oscar Wilde, Manet, Picasso, and Verlaine had all been notorious absinthe enthusiasts. Baudelaire once said of it: "If you would not feel the horrible burden of Time that breaks your shoulders and bows you to the earth, you must intoxicate yourself unceasingly." Maybe this was it, the reason we all drank it, and the reason we were all here. I envisioned some of their works— Degas' *L'Absinthe*, a stunned pair sitting in a booth before a glass, shoulders slumped, expressions far away. Or Picasso's

3

The Absinthe Drinker, a gaunt woman with sunken features and talon-like hands hunched over her glass in a dark-hued portrait of addiction. How the masters would have painted this place, I thought and shuddered. I imagined their canvases filled with the vacant eyes and fallen features of the absinthe users of this town. A town that had taken to its breast something that was more than merely illegal but which was also dangerous and taboo.

I had arrived in a place where nothing was taboo.

"Sign it," an intruder demanded, interrupting my reverie, causing me to lift my head. I realized I had fallen into a gentle waking sleep, into absinthe's diaphanous arms once again. "Sign it," the intruder repeated, thrusting a Kraft envelope at my face. I signed a flapping carbon paper slip held on by a piece of clear tape. "What's the signature say?" The man squinted at the receipt.

"Pitch. Nathan Pitch." I said.

"You the story editor?" he asked.

"That's right."

He leaned onto a pile of scripts, and with irritation printed my name clearly beneath my signature as his pocket pager went off. It sounded like a scream in my head so raw from drink. He left me with a snarl and went on to his next delivery.

I instantly knew by the package's weight that it would supersede everything stacked on my desk. Tearing into it, I saw it was no mere trifle of a screenplay, but a soon-to-be-published book. A hot manuscript. Attached was a note from Chick Bell, one of the studio's creative executives.

WORMWOOD

Nathan,
Enclosed is No Rewards for the Deserving, *a new*
manuscript by Weissbrot. We need coverage on it by
tomorrow.
Best, Chickie.

With the last remnants of my work ethic, I attacked the hefty tome, reading straight through lunch and into the early evening. All the stories in this town had to be read, and that was my job at the studio. When scripts came in, as they did countless times every day, I would either assign it to a reader or read it myself if it was important enough. I read like a draft horse pulled and did not complain about the workload. I suspect this was why I was still around. Once, I had had the knack for picking and passing correctly on projects, and had become the go-to guy in the studio's Story Department. For the past several months I had read poorly photocopied text all day long, until my eyes were permanently pinched in a squint. I read parts or the whole of over two thousand screenplays, books, teleplays, outlines, and treatments from Nobel laureates right on down to burger flippers and valet parking attendants. Of these works, perhaps ten, not ten percent but ten, were in various stages of being made into films. Of those few, perhaps three warranted it. Unlike others in my position, I actually read what I commented on, and perhaps this is what had originally made me valuable to the studio. I had managed to make myself their little gem, their rocking horse winner. The more I read and commented on, the more they gave me to read. I had never minded the volume, though, for I was a reader for

5

a living, a good pro. But then the lies and the fear and the absinthe seeped in, and I could no longer shield my true opinion from my own politically motivated one.

This was the case with the particular book in front of me. I did not know where I stood on it or what I should tell the studio to this end. The book was an important one. I'd dare call it literature in certain circles. The studio wasn't one of these circles, however. A literary achievement wasn't of much concern to a studio if it wouldn't yield a blockbuster movie. This book, about a boy's choice of the wrong path—away from family and religion, toward moral bankruptcy—was not filmic. The main character ended up working in the film industry, where all sorts of outlandish happenings led him to debase himself irreparably. It was dark comedy laced with bittersweet tragedy. This subject, though, was just not appropriate for the company. A belles lettres character drama—critics' fare with limited box-office potential—was not the type of movie the studio made, I decided, and so I said when I wrote up my thoughts on it that night.

It wasn't Weissbrot, the writer's, fault, but there had been several laughing images released of late that had been set in this, the very town in which movies were made. They had parodied or satirized elements of the business, and they had all gone too far. They evoked the blatant superficiality and commercialism of things here, and did so with faint hints of accuracy, but they all had a plot twist—a murder, an outlandish business coup—that was divorced from reality. The problem was, they caricatured something that was already exaggerated. If a writer, and Weissbrot seemed to know this, wanted to send up or run down the town, all he really had to do was tell the truth about it. Weissbrot had done so, but that didn't mean his book was going to sell, or be made into a movie. It meant, in fact, the opposite.

I stayed at work late into the night finishing my summary, which neatly neutered and encapsulated within two and a half pages what it had probably taken Weissbrot years to get down. I went ahead and checked off the "box score," which made coverage even quicker to read.

	Excellent	Good	Fair	Poor
Premise			...X	
Plotline			X....	
Characters	X...			
Dialogue	X...			
Structure	X...			
Setting			...X	

Project Recommendation: PASS
Writer Recommendation: PASS—too good for this place
Concept Recommendation: Forget about it.

I recognized the absurdity in what I was doing—writing a summary of a summary of a summary—when it dawned on me that there was a category missing. One that stood above the rest as far as the studio was concerned. I went ahead and added it.

Greed
Potential: Weak

What more did they really want to know?

It was four-thirty in the morning when I finished and my phone rang. My caller identification readout told me it was Jumper Sussman, the president of the studio, on the line.

"Nathan, you got it, star?" came Sussman's voice through a cloud of cigar smoke that I could fairly hear.

"Yes, Jumper," I answered. "I've got it right here. You want it between breakfasts?" I asked. No powerful executive had less than two breakfast meetings on any given day.

"Fax me," Jumper puffed.

"Done," I stated.

"You're the man," the chief offered.

I exceeded him. "No, *you're* the man, Jumper." This was ritual. It was as necessary to Jumper's sense of well-being as his rolling a Havana between thumb and forefinger and sniffing it, before clipping the end and lighting up.

"That's right, kid, but you're the star," Jumper last-worded me and hung up. There was a time when I had deserved this title which he conferred on me, back when I could rip through a piece of material and turn around coverage on it within an hour or two tops and had believed my job important. Now it took me nearly five times as long, thanks to my shimmering green mistress.

Before sending the fax, I opened my desk drawer and arranged its contents on my desktop. The pages sat in the machine, waiting to be sent through, but I eyed the sugar cubes, the strainer spoon, the heavy triangular-shaped glass, and label-less bottle in front of me. I had my own ritual, one for which I could no longer wait. I poured four fingers of absinthe from the bottle, lay the strainer across the rim of the glass, and placed a few sugar cubes upon it. I drizzled cool water over the sugar, which began breaking down into an opaque mush and dissolved into the glass. The verdant liquid lightened in color and turned cloudy and opalescent. Stirring in more cool spring water, I removed the strainer and drank the first bracing sip. My nose opened as it would over a can of paint thinner. The substance entered my bloodstream, a high-voltage jolt of heavy alcohol and various herbs which blended to form a potent narcotic. The result was a soothing sensation that eased the knot of tension in my neck. As I drank, I previewed in my mind what would happen here tomorrow:

When I sent the fax, Jumper Sussman would get the feel for Weissbrot's book from my synopsis. I would receive a stern memo about my "greed potential" jab before Jumper would, of course, concur with my assessment. The book was a pass. The producer, Foster Miles, who had submitted it to the studio, however, had given us an advance peek at the work, and Chick Bell would want to capitalize on that. To discard a secretly submitted piece would be a waste. Chick would slip a copy of my report to a high-ranking executive at a different studio, and another copy to a parallel development executive at yet another studio who often sent over opinions from her own Nathan Pitch-type.

The development executive, not feeling the piece appropriate either, would sling the coverage over to a crosstown studio boss who might like it. Information on a project that had been rejected but was not widely known was a way to curry favor with an executive. This was a wise thing to do, since one would no doubt be working with, or for, those whom one curried before long. All parties knew that the piece in question was useless, for a valuable project would never be shown around so indiscriminately, but this was not the point. This system let one know who one's friends were. Alas, after farming out the synopsis to his own stable of producers, who would not feel the material fetching either, the crosstown studio boss would decline with careful consideration. One of these producers from his stable, though, thinking it prudent, would run it by fax to an old co-worker now at another studio. . . . In this way the entire town would appreciate and ignore a fine work that, although soon to be featured in the *New York Times Book Review* with glowing praise, would be read by me alone.

The system hadn't always been so clear to me. In the beginning I had not understood what was happening around me, for I still cared deeply about things like doing a good job, and succeeding and being well liked and regarded. But those concerns had faded now that I knew how the business worked. It spun slowly, like a colossal grist mill, crushing and grinding everything in its path into the fine dust of ransomed humanity and failure. I was now aware of the two types who escaped it: those who abandoned their humanity and so rose to such stature that the wheel could not roll over them, and it was rather they who stopped the wheel in its track. And those so amorphous, so chameleon-like, or so insignificant, that they may be passed over by a pit in the wheel's surface and left untouched until it passed again. As a younger man there was little question of which type I aimed to be, while now I had no doubt as to which I had become.

I continued drinking as the night ran out, reaching the place on the bottle where the label would have been if it were a store-bought concoction, and then went below that. With each glass I used less water and less sugar, upping the octane of my mixture as I could tolerate the 140 proof—70 percent alcohol level—of the absinthe. I stared at the wall and considered how I had originally come here to claim my place, to become a producer of the laughing images, a creative force. Before I had even arrived, I had assumed I would automatically belong once I did. Now, though, the days had become tough to get through, and I was plagued by a constant low-grade fever and waking dreams of full bottles that pursued me until I was crawling out of my skin. Like all the rest, I had arrived innocent, enthusiastic, suffused with youthful notions of having something to say, and wanting to earn a living making films that said it. Another fool wanting desperately to crack the club-like exclusivity of the business, and willing to do whatever it took. Now the innocence was a soiled memory, the going not so easy, and I longed only for freedom. Freedom from my desk and this system to which I was shackled, freedom from story and summary and words. I wanted to speak without apology, to spare no thought for studio politics. I wanted only to do things for their own sake, and without thought of some hidden end.

In a bleary haze I drank on into the dawn, until my bottle was done. I looked at the drained vessel with a feeling of panic—panic that emptying an entire bottle in a night was even possible for me, and panic that now my bottle was empty. I felt a moment's sickening vertigo and put my head down on my desk to stabilize. I had been in my office for close to twenty-four hours, and awake for days, but when I closed my eyes sleep was still far off.

There had been nights at the beginning when I was too excited to sleep. Instead I would drive to the studio and walk around the back lots for a while and then read scripts in my office until morning when everyone else arrived. Now sleep was a corrosive state. Each time I closed my eyes at home there came turbulent dreams—a vicious side effect of absinthe. One dream in particular recurred. In it I had the sensation of hovering above and looking down upon myself on the bed. I would see an ancient, crag-faced man of the Far East approach my sleeping form and drive his elbow into my stomach in a precise way. He would methodically burst each of my internal organs, one after another, rupturing my spleen, rending my gallbladder, tearing my liver, preserving my heart for last. I would simply lie there in wonder, accepting the brutality, until he moved in for his finish. Only then would I roll into action and drive knife-like fingers into the man's throat and each of his eyes. A mysterious, beautiful woman would then enter the scene and nonchalantly greet me and the ancient man as the blood and gore ran down our hands. The dream defied any analysis I could apply. With such a panorama awaiting me, sleep was pushed beyond the realm of the possible. Eventually I stopped returning home much at all, and spent most dawns, like this one, at the studio, no longer out of joy or enthusiasm but out of paralysis.

At last I lifted my head, shoved myself away from my desk, and guided myself toward the door with a hand against the wall. Already I could hear the sound of muted "good mornings" and computers and printers and photocopiers and shredders humming to life around me. I stepped out of the building hoping for a fresh breath of morning air. Instead I got a lung's worth of hot, cinder-filled stuff that had blown in off the desert to the east. There was a reflecting pool at the foot of The Bunker, and I made my way to it and sat down on the edge. This was where I watched the rising sun illuminate a heavy opaque sky every morning. The light grew pink-gray on the pollution-fat clouds until it appeared that the underbelly of Jupiter was pressing down on the city, the studio, and myself.

Soon a serpentine line of cars began to bleed into the parking structure. I watched them arrive, each piloted by a solo driver, a new entrant in the derby. If they were like me, and I just like them, then I was supposed to have compassion for them, for their situation, for it all. But I no longer did. All they wanted was to get in and stay in, to live well, or to sleep, and it made me disgusted with myself for feeling the same way. I searched my memory for something useful I might have been taught—from my father with his noble theories, or from the professors at my fine college—an idea or philosophy that would help me care again about my fellow toilers. But there was nothing.

I looked down into the black water of the reflecting pool and was vaguely frightened by what I saw there—a gaunt, dull-eyed creature, with a forbidding, if not pained, expression across the mouth and cheeks, who shimmered as if painted by Van Gogh. I reached in and splashed some of the fetid water on my face, as much to disperse my own image as to wake myself up. The cars had stopped arriving, and the glare had grown painfully bright around me. It prodded me to go back inside. I dried my hands on my pants and stood. I had several meetings to attend—at any of which I could expect to be finally, roughly, and irrevocably fired, to be cut off from everything I'd ever wanted and worked for. Then, all at once, I decided. If it was far too late to save myself, perhaps it was not too late to save Weissbrot's beautiful book. I hunched my shoulders with resolve and moved back toward my office to rewrite the coverage. I would call Weissbrot's book the ripest screen prospect I'd ever seen. Maybe the film rights would sell, maybe I'd be executed, but I intended to at least make a terrible mess. I smiled grimly to myself as I entered the building. I hadn't foreseen any of this when I had arrived here; back then all I had wanted was a job.

My first job was in the mailroom of ACE—Associated Creative Endeavors—a large literary and talent agency where I pushed a cart while I awaited entry into their training program. I had come to town from Queens, New York, with a car full of clothes and a crisp new college diploma. A "sheepskin," my father called it. I had no idea that everybody else in town already had that much and more. "It's all about who you know in that business," it had been impressed upon me by my father, who came from the hard-work-will-yield-reward school of business thought. Also impressed upon me by him was that I had every tool I could possibly need, that by simply showing

up, plugging myself in, and adding the indomitable enthusiasm and drive that were considered to be my birthright, I
couldn't help but be a huge, splashy success in short order.
The morning I left on my cross-country drive, he pressed a
piece of paper into my hand.

"Here are a few contacts, old friends from the club who
have connections. Look them up as soon as you get there."
His short sentences were packed with much meaning: I was
to get to work right away upon my arrival; there was to be no
messing around. I was to do as he said. The subtext was that
after growing up poor, he was now a member of a country club
where even as he worked on his golf swing he endeavored to
further his son's opportunities.

"Thanks."

"There's this too." He handed me a wrinkled envelope. It
contained a thousand dollars. "You won't need anything else,"
he told me in a way that discouraged the idea of asking for
more in the future.

"Thanks." We stood uncomfortably. I did not know if this
was a hug or a handshake occasion. He extended a hand. I
supposed there was no such thing as a hug occasion.

"Remember T. Boone, boy." He spoke through the open car
window as I got in and started it up, invoking the name of
one of the self-made heroes to whom he religiously referred.

"I'll be a studio executive within a year," I stated, putting
the car into gear. As I drove away from my father's upraised
thumb, I could practically hear his oft-repeated treatise on the
career.

"First you get your feet wet," he'd tell me. "Then, in your

thirties you secure your position within the corporate structure. First to arrive, last to leave. Every day. Your forties are
when you will rise—garner a presidency or CEO status—and
in your fifties you'll make your move. Flip companies, make
massive stock sell-offs. No fucking prisoners." I would nod
and take it all in as if we wouldn't be speaking again until
after I was finished executing the entire plan. I was twenty-
one and had no real idea of what even the getting-my-feet-wet
part would entail.

The actual plugging in, the obtaining of a job, any job, at
which to apply myself with Vince Lombardi-like zeal, was
difficult. Distastefully more so than it was supposed to have
been. Strangely, my father's list of contacts was exhausted
quite quickly. Two of the people on it called him back, not
understanding my message, before telling him they could not
help me. Another was retired, and the other three did not take
my call. The thousand bucks was a memory, and I was making
a poor effort at waiting on tables by the time I finally scored
my low-level entry post. I responded to a classified advertise-
ment and showed up at the ACE agency for a mass interview
on a Tuesday.

I sat in a cavernous cafeteria surrounded by dozens of pro-
spective candidates who looked so similar to me that my mind
raced for a way of distinguishing myself. We were given a
battery of diagnostic tests—typing, knowledge of city streets,
a sort of moral multi-phasic that could only have been to determine if a candidate might steal office supplies. I waited six
hours for a personal interview with a grizzled senior agent. As

I sat, I tried to foresee specific questions he might ask and practiced witty and wise responses to them. But when I was finally called, the interview went so fast that none of my prepared answers applied. We weren't from the same place, hadn't gone to the same school, and I hadn't joined a fraternity at all, much less the one he'd been in. It didn't look promising for me. Toward the end, as the agent checked my contact phone number and his watch, his phone rang. He spoke briefly about a script he had recently sold. "Sea Wolf" was the title. He hung up, and I blurted out a question.

"Is it based on the Jack London novel?" I did not consider if he would appreciate my eavesdropping. His heavy-lidded eyes twitched upward.

"You know the Jack London novel?" he asked with intense interest. I nodded. "You must be extremely well read."

I shrugged and looked at him. The way he said it, I felt he might be insulting me. Instead he picked up my résumé from the tall stack it had been in and looked it over. "Tell me," he said, peering over at me, "do you really want to be an agent?"

—Here it is, I thought, a chance. I felt the gears and mechanisms in my mind lurch to high-speed life. The only answer he wanted was yes. Otherwise the agency would not waste its resources training a person who was just going to end up elsewhere. The truth was, I did not want to be an agent, to spend my career peddling the talents of others for ten percent. The truth was that I wanted to produce. I wanted to work at a studio first, to learn the process from the inside before going out on my own to spend my days on movie sets working closely with writers, directors, and actors. Then, after many successful films I wanted to return to a studio and run it. To make all the important decisions. But to even hint at these aspirations would have sounded imbecilic. It was well known that the agency route was the fastest way to a studio job which led to the rest. The shrewd play was to get into a training program, garner contacts, and hopefully achieve agent status briefly before making a vertical move to production. So, did I want to be an agent?

"Yes," I answered, looking into his tiny eyes, "I want nothing more." He marked my résumé and put it in the small pile.

"Next Monday, seven fifteen A.M. Wear a tie," he said, before yelling "Next" over my shoulder.

The agency was housed in an ornate white marble building at the foot of the Beverly Hills. Sharply suited men and women with shining hair came and went from their assigned parking spaces bearing Filofaxes and cellular phones, bringing along with them the business of the town. Although I was the low man on a very tall totem pole, my sails were filled by getting a job at a distinguished place like ACE. I entered the offices early my first morning and was delivered into the hands of Jared, the man in charge of the mailroom. Jared, who spoke in a precise lisping way, was bald, hook-nosed, and tanned to a deep nut brown color. Without ceremony he put me with the others who sorted the incoming mail and placed it on carts. All in their early twenties and cadaverously pale, my coworkers and I were each assigned a specific route through the maze of cubicles and glass-walled offices on which to steer our carts. By 8:30 A.M. Jared clapped loudly to quiet us so he could formally address the new trainees. The room grew silent as he cleared his throat and adjusted his expression.

"This is the 'hole' "—he gestured at the mailroom—"and it is my domain. You will find I am a stern and perhaps not just god. But I get paid to make this place run. You will be allowed only the allotted breaks—see your employee hand-books—and I will not stand for any delays on the mail runs. If you are late and have an excuse less serious than colon cancer, that disease will seem like a blessing by the time I get finished with you."

My stomach dropped at what I was hearing. I glanced around at my cohorts for a sign that he might be joking. The new trainees were grave and white around the mouth. Those who had been in the mailroom for a while merely looked down.

"Personal phone calls will earn you a reprimand and a no-tation in your file," Jared continued, the *s* and *f* sounds jump-ing off his lips like fat from sizzling bacon. He went on for fifteen minutes, in a tightly rehearsed way, about demeanor, personal grooming, language, attitude, and the off-limits na-ture of all clerical supplies. The idea of using the company postal machine for even a single piece of private correspon-dence was sheer lunacy. I suddenly saw with clarity what my college degree was worth in the working world. Welcome to the hole.

After the morning sorting and delivery my hands were a mass of tiny, stinging paper cuts. We took care of outgoing mail in the afternoons, as well as the copying of scripts and other materials, and any demeaning personal matters, it seemed, the agents could think of having Jared assign. Taking an agent's car to be washed or collecting his dry cleaning was commonplace. A mailroom boy had to go out and buy shoes for one agent's daughter, eyebrow wax for another. The break in routine that these chores provided was quite well balanced by the inherent humiliation factor in carrying them out. There was no such thing as commiseration either. By the time I had spent a few days in the hole, I saw that I would make no friends there. It was all about competition. Politically speaking, keeping to oneself and not threatening Jared were the only ways to bide time while awaiting assignment to an agent's desk as an assistant. The only way to distinguish oneself was by not distinguishing oneself in the negative.

In my vivid imagination, the business was to have been exciting conversations about the deeper meanings of movie scenes with French directors, parties held in hilltop houses, comparisons of acting methods and cinematographers, visits to interesting locations, the odd klieg-lit premiere, all on the way toward whopping producing fees and back-end profit participation. . . . I read about these perquisites in the trades, saw evidence of them spilling out of restaurants, driving by in expensive cars, wafting along in snippets of cell-phone conversations. This side of the business seemed to exist in a parallel dimension to mine, though—nearby but off limits to me.

Every morning, noon, and night the agents above ground would submit head shots, résumés, videotapes, and screenplays to casting directors, producers, and studios. Three times a day I would traverse the halls behind my mail cart, picking up the seeds and fruits of their labors. On these runs I learned what I could of agenting, which was little, save that I would need expensive suits with boxy jackets and baggy-cut pants, and colorful, asymmetrically patterned ties, should I eventually be promoted to their level. I saw them work the phones, looking for the next hot project, the upcoming star, the cash-rich buyer, the quickly unfolding deal. I sensed that true talent was a lagging second to good hype. I learned that reading a phone sheet upside down off somebody's desk was important, but not nearly as crucial as simply lying well. I learned that while information was princely, rumor was king.

I pushed my cart and kept my sensors open and my feelers out. One thing I noticed quickly, hints of it even on my first nervous morning, was the sexual orientation of the agency. I had recently come from a small New England college where sexual rights and freedoms were popular social issues. Live and let live and let's all be friends. And I agreed. In theory. The office population of ACE presented itself as totally heterosexual with some gregariously asexual folks thrown in. Yet, on a daily basis, I'd encounter Paul Scarano. Scarano was a tall, willowy junior agent who spoke with a more pronounced lisp than Jared but went on ceaselessly about "banging broads" and "boating bangtail." It was difficult for me to buy into what he said next to what my gut told me about him. There was also Trudy McGreevy, a top talent handler, who was close to three hundred pounds, a heavily mustached woman who laughed with a deep, throaty "huh-huh-huh." And Carter Percy, a mid-level rep in the literary department, who was from Georgia and tried to play the married and mannered southern gentleman, but who I had caught staring me up and down more than once while he decorously fingered his Van

Dyke. It became increasingly clear to me that the real break-down of the place was in fact a mix of the homosexual, bitterly asexual, and only somewhat heterosexual. It was something that should not have mattered in a professional environment, but as the agents, assistants, secretaries, messengers, office managers, and the like bustled throughout the halls, they gave off the strained air of unconvincing liars. All these supposed mainstream professionals were dragging the weight of their divided personal lives through the office halls. They were a group of individuals forced to tuck away their own propensities for a good part of their day and instead cling to a nebulous mainstream identity. It made human dealings unnatural and hinted at the unhealthy. Relationships reeked of the hidden. There was the time Trudy was telling an actress she represented about The Palms. It's a "hell of a dyke bar . . ." she said, and carefully added, "though I've never been there myself." Coursing the halls behind my mail cart, I had to deal with all manner of approaches, from a few instances of genuine warmth to strafing runs from Ben Mack, someone I deduced as the office queen, but who would turn blue denying the assertion. Maybe I was too sensitive, but I felt a subtle yet undeniable glow of enmity directed toward me because I didn't bear the burden they did. As I grew accustomed to the climate of the office, I could not shake the feeling that many around me were hiding, cowering really, and resented me for not needing to do so as well.

After a month on the job I decided not to leave it to chance encounter but to conscientiously meet every single agent at the agency. I broke up the timing of my mail runs so that when an assistant left his or her cubicle, I would go to that office with a question for the agent if he or she "wasn't too busy."

"Excuse me, sir, anything else going out?" I'd peek in, possibly receiving a hostile wave away but sometimes getting a "Not right now, say, you're new . . ."

"I'm Nathan Pitch,"

"Hiya, hiya, hiya."

As soon as a few knew me, and I greeted them in passing or waved hello, others started making introductions to me as well. Just a mail kid, but the agents didn't want to be scooped by their cohorts, that just wouldn't do, such a competitive industry and all. For all they knew, my uncle ran a studio.

One of the agents I met was a thirty-year-old woman named Shelby Stark. I was making my afternoon sweep when I came upon an empty assistant's cubicle. Nudging open the adjoining office door with an "Excuse me, is there anything going out?" I came upon a crying woman who might have been attractive had she been a veterinarian, a teacher, or even an attorney. But she bore the hardened and hollowed-out aspect which I had found to be common in all agents, and which disturbed her technically attractive features.

"I'm sorry. I . . . Is my assistant out there?" she said, as vulnerable as I would ever see her.

"No," I answered.

"Oh . . . shit," she said, sobbing a little.

I pulled back my cart, preparing to leave, but instead asked, "Are you all right?" She brightened, like a dying flower receiving sunlight. "Is there anything I can do for you?" I continued. She looked a bit startled; apparently another's show of concern wasn't a commom occurrence in this office.

She had me sit down and related a story, the first of many that people would volunteer to me in a town that fed on stories. I must have been so inconsequential to her that she couldn't see the harm in telling me that she was afraid she would lose her job because she had been seen having lunch with an old college friend who worked at a smaller agency. She feared her bosses would think she was looking for another job and preemptively fire her for her transgression. I listened with all the compassion I could muster.

"Let it be known you were just trading information. Nobody would switch from ACE to that agency unless they had to," I said. "It seems like common sense . . ."

She moved a tissue away from her reddened nose and glared. "Well, that's the first thing that goes in this business."

A silent moment passed between us, and I watched as she puzzled it out. "You're . . . right . . . though. I think," she allowed, "I'll play it like I was just sharing information to get information." She began to straighten in her chair. A subtle connection was growing between us. "So you're new around here. Tell me about yourself."

I spoke of my aspirations in the few minutes I knew were being allotted to me. By the time I left her office Shelby thanked me profusely, but I had fallen behind on my route and was four minutes late getting back to the mailroom.

"What took you so long?" Jared asked accusingly.

Swept away in my own benevolent ability to help others, I answered guilelessly, "I was talking to one of the agents. She was upset..." As Jared heard this, his whole countenance changed, and I knew at once I had made a mistake.

"Really?" Jared hissed in his smug, drawn-out way. "I thought you were supposed to be delivering mail, not counseling agents."

Idiot, idiot, idiot, I repeated to myself. All these weeks in the mailroom, lying low and trying only to shine wasted.

"I've got something else for you to do," Jared continued. "You'll be my new runner. That'll keep you out of the agents' way."

I suddenly resented Shelby Stark and her tears and wanted to dash Jared over the head with a laptop. Most of all I wanted to tear at myself for my own foolish sentiment. How the hell could one be demoted from the mailroom? And yet I had found a way.

"Which agent was upset?" Jared asked greedily.

"It's not important." I blanked him, which did not make him happy.

"What are you, some wealth of personal feeling?" he prodded. "Do you really care if someone's upset?" He snorted at me. "You'll never make it in this business," the little mole of a man said, as if he were the one to make such pronouncements. Stuck in his hole forever, he considered himself a success in show biz, an executive even.

"I disagree," was all I said, walking out toward the men's bathroom to splash cold water on my face.

• • •

Jared preened the next day. Wielding his power, he sent me driving manila envelopes and pursuing senseless tasks east, west, north, and south. Along my way I considered the man and what *his* goals might have been. What had happened to him to make him this way? A bitterness flowed from him, not from a deep, tragic wound, but rather, it roiled along his surface like winds across a desolate planet. Jared assigned awful, degrading tasks to hardworking, educated people, and did so with glee. All those who had been promoted out of the mailroom and had gone on to better jobs and better lives while he had to stay had made him bitter. The man lived to see people fall, to make them miserable when they did, and now I had drawn his attention to myself.

I was assigned a pager and had to drive around packages on a tight schedule. No sooner would I have battled traffic, finally located an office, and gained the required signature on something when my pager would sound. I would have to locate a working phone and call in, only to have another pickup or delivery assigned. As hard as the other messengers worked, Jared had me working harder. I could feel it in the way he barked out instructions. "When you're done over there, get to the Valley for a pickup. Pronto. Thank you so very much, Nathan."

The pager, that contemptible piece of electronics, quickly became the bane of my existence. I was instructed to take it home with me at night, and when I objected, Jared told me to take it home weekends as well. That night I took it home with me but kept it turned off. The next day Jared said, "I paged you last night at ten-thirty. Why didn't you answer?"

"It must be broken," I answered, obviously lying.

"If that thing isn't answered within two minutes from now on, you're fired," he threatened me.

As I drove around in bottleneck traffic, insidious heat steamed off the blacktop and up through the floorboards of my car, and it became difficult for me to connect the way I spent my days with the dreams I had brought to this town. I knew another runner, one who had started only a month or two before me, and he was gone now. He had recently come unwound while stuck in a traffic jam. Stomping on the accelerator, he had smashed into the car in front of him, then put it in reverse and crashed into the car behind him. He had done it again and again, continuing until the car he was driving had been destroyed. He had returned home to North Carolina and started selling paper products. His story sent a prickling finger of recognition up my spine. I saw how the lower rungs of the business served to break one down. The time one had to move up was not unlimited. Surrender and failure waited like implacable vultures for any breakdown. My situation was not a personal thing between Jared and me, but rather the way business was conducted at the agency. All who could were dishing out spiteful abuses in order to knock their subordinates further down. People were not simply working for their own success, but to see others fail. I was drawing some pretty bad details, we all were. After the pager exchange, though, I felt Jared put just a bit more thought into sending me on the unsavory runs. Like the day of the flamingos.

• • •

I was sent to the hilltop home of a producer known in town for his eccentricities. He was an older gentleman, and I was surprised when he answered the door himself, as I had never actually met anyone above domestic servant or personal assistant level on my deliveries. The man was perhaps seventy, but had undergone a few surgical facial tightenings, so I could not be sure. He had curly hair the color and texture of steel wool and was clad in a silk brocade robe. He led me in and excused himself. I stood in his richly appointed living room and took in the decor. Sofas and armchairs stuffed to rotundity created a conversation pit around a marble coffee table topped by several orchid plants. The carpet beneath my feet was soft and lushly patterned. This seemed to be the very site of one of my many imagined show business gatherings, where in my mind I traded bon mots with the leaders of the industry. I looked out the bay window through which I saw a pool and patio area strewn with dozens of pink flamingos of all different sizes and materials. I drifted over to get a better look at the birds. Some were latex, balloon-like; others were spray-painted styrofoam; one even seemed to be an actual taxidermied bird standing on one leg in the shallow end of the pool. The turquoise water and the neon pink flamingos blended together to pleasing effect. Also strewn around the pool were a platoon of boys, most younger than myself.

My gut feeling was to bolt, but something other than waiting for the delivery receipt—morbid curiosity perhaps—rooted me to the spot where I stood. The old man's arrival back in the room seemed to confirm my initial instinct, for now he was stark naked—except for a heavy braided gold chain around his neck—and he was quite shriveled. He was so wrinkled that the folds of his skin seemed to form secret pouches where messages could be stashed. The image of his body covered with long-forgotten folded correspondence and delivery receipts was strong impulse for me to smile. I bridled it with all the control I possessed. I felt certain that to smile or laugh right at that moment would tilt the situation irretrievably off its axis and send it spinning beyond the surreal.

Abruptly the old man thrust out the now signed delivery receipt and a hundred-dollar bill as a tip and shrugged. It was logical, after all, his nakedness being the only incongruity to the transaction. I took the slip and waved off the tip. I suddenly felt light-headed and my vision went a bit spotty, and so was unprepared when the man asked, "Do you have to get back right away? Or can you join us for a drink by the pool?"

The question was clear enough, and yes, it seemed to me, getting in my car right now and driving back in the heat and traffic seemed impossible. "A glass of water," I answered.

"Out by the pool," the old man said, ushering me out, sliding open the bay window.

I followed him dumbly, as the sound of gentle splashing and muted conversation reached my ears. I was surprised at the hushed tones, as visually the scene connoted a good deal more frolic. Along one side of the pool stood a lavish buffet. A formally dressed waiter paced its length with a spray bottle, lazily misting sliced fruit and vegetables. Now behind the wet bar, the old man nudged aside an indifferent attendant and poured me a glass of water. I gulped it as if it were the first

I'd ever had, and then paused, standing there wiping my mouth, almost trying to hide behind the glass.

"If you'd like to stay, we have trunks, or . . ." the old man offered, as I realized that some of the handsome young men had selected the latter, unspoken option. A few of the more rambunctious of them were engaged in a pecking contest in the water, using a couple of flamingos of the inflatable variety. I simply took one step backward, and then another, until I reached the plate-glass wall I had just passed through a moment before. The old man stepped out from behind the wet bar, his genitals swinging comically, and stared at me with the woeful eyes of a steer as I slid open the door. I quickly crossed the living room and left through the front door. I was already in my car before I realized I still held the glass from which I had just drunk.

After leaving the producer's house I drove around the hills for a while, becoming lost in the winding canyon roads before finally emerging onto Sunset. At last recognizing my surroundings, I piloted my car west and toward my home. I finally admitted it to myself—to me, the business was like an unfamiliar bazaar in a strange Middle Eastern country. I wondered how much longer I could remain at my job doing these kinds of deliveries before I too found myself ramming into something over and over in bewildered frustration. I arrived at my cheaply constructed and pink-painted building—the first time I had done so in daylight on a weekday since I had begun working at ACE four and a half months earlier—and went inside. I was expected back in the mailroom, but I could not

bring myself to return. Instead I called in with an excuse of
food poisoning and pushed the thought of consequences out
of my head. I lay down on my bed and looked out over the
sterility of my inexpensively furnished bachelor-sized apartment. The ceiling above me was dimpled like medium-curd
cottage cheese. The walls were thin enough to hear a neighbor
cough through. It was the kind of place that had never looked
new for a moment, that had probably seemed old by the end
of its first week. I lived in all the luxury that a cracker did
within its box. This was my cracker box.

I looked across the room to the steady red light of my empty
answering machine. I had been spending all my time alone
since my move to town and had no friends here to call. The
business, which had begun to grow dark and strange to me,
was my only companion. I thought of calling my father on the
East Coast, but had no idea what I would say. He wouldn't
understand, really wouldn't believe, the things I'd already
seen. It seemed his world of business was a logical theater of
operations most often viewed in old 1950s movies where
square-suited men returned from the office on the 5:15 to
wives and pot roasts. I considered calling my mother on her
little farm in the middle of the country. She was even further
away from understanding where I was at, though. I wondered
how they had ever been married in the first place. I had one
memory of them together from when I was a child. I had come
home from kindergarten with a beautiful flower, a tiger lily,
for my mother. On impulse I had picked it from a neighbor's
garden on the way home from school because I wanted to give
her something nice. It must have been obvious to her where

I got it, for she accepted it with an expression of concern before putting it in water. Later, when my father arrived home from work, he saw the flower and asked where it had come from. When he heard the answer, he pulled it from the vase, shoved it at me, and said, "You take this back to the neighbors' and apologize for stealing. . . ." He began throwing ice cubes into a glass and reached for a liquor bottle. My mother began to cry. He always had right on his side and took everything he wanted—including me in the divorce—and she was too sensitive for her own good. It seemed my mother, father, and myself were from three separate planets altogether. I walked halfway to the neighbors' that night, then threw the flower down and buried it.

I chose against dialing up anyone, and instead closed my eyes and pictured returning home to New York for a premiere screening of a film I had produced, or better yet, anonymously watching it in the back of a theater and gauging the audience's reaction from my own seat. . . . I was hardly closer to it now than when I had arrived, but I now knew at least one thing for certain—that I had to get out of the mailroom. Soon. I vowed that I would figure a way out.

Early the morning after the flamingo incident, the whole crew was in the mailroom having coffee or a cigarette. It was before the mail had arrived, and we were all trying to enjoy a waking moment when Jared or an agent wasn't ordering us around or simply berating us, when a smooth, feral-looking man in a well-cut suit of supple blue mohair entered. He gazed around the place in a wistful yet knowing manner. The look on his suntanned face was equal parts nostalgia and disgust. Those of us who were going to get anywhere in the business knew the man as Mickey Kessler, a top agent, a partner at ACE. Jared walked in, and he and Kessler conferred discreetly for a moment, all of our eyes averted yet upon them. Kessler gestured toward me, and Jared shook his head emphatically. Kessler nodded his own head with more emphasis and then left. When he was gone, Jared approached me with agitation.

"Nathan, you don't look very sick," he accused.

"It passed," I said, meeting his gaze, "but believe me, I was—"

"Well, I've got a little something for you to do," he said. "Meet Mr. Kessler—that's the gentleman who just left—in his office." As I made to go, a few of the most veteran mailroomers snickered.

"Lifers," I said aloud, silencing the giggling baboons as I left, happy to be doing anything other than driving around in traffic for the moment.

The agent Mickey Kessler was well known in the industry, partially for his ruthless deal making, and also for the ancient, overstuffed leather chair he kept in his office. The chair was completely tattered, shredded, and had stuffing exploding from hundreds of lacerations. It was supposed to be a complete eyesore in an otherwise immaculately decorated office, but the chair was not for sitting. It seemed Kessler, pent up from his many important daily pressures, exorcised his demons by bull-whipping the innocent piece of furniture in some sado-macho show of edginess. The agent had also cut an admirable swath of big-time deals behind him, receiving a seven-figure salary and six-figure bonuses.

I was full of nerves as I approached his office. I knew this could be my chance to make it onto a desk. In the training program I would begin to learn the business behind the creative process—who the players were, how deals were made, how movie packages were put together. I was fantasizing about how I would say good-bye forever to Jared as I stopped in front of a beleaguered young guy who sat outside Kessler's office.

"My name's Nathan Pitch. From the mailroom," I began.

The young man with dark circles beneath his eyes cut me off. "Go right in."

Inside the glass-walled office, Mickey Kessler was pacing around, speaking on the telephone through a headset. He looked like a well-dressed, somewhat possessed, air-traffic controller. He motioned for me to have a seat. Behind the desk, toward the corner, I saw the famed whipping chair, sliced a hundred times over, looking like some sad, kept pet. The horsehide weapon itself lay coiled on top of Kessler's phone call return sheet. The agent was in the midst of seducing a writer to sign with the agency. As Kessler paced, chest puffed out, he shouted into the headset mouthpiece. "Listen, you sign on here and we'll work *with* you on your scripts. We practically do development in-house. We understand artists. I'm an agent, but I still consider myself a filmmaker." I listened, noting his convincing style, while he went on to discuss a meeting and transferred the call out to his assistant for scheduling. I waited expectantly until Kessler clicked off the phone and turned to me.

"That was a hot young writer—a freshman at USC—I'm going to sign. . . . Anyway, my wife's in this room at the L'Ermitage," Kessler said, flipping me a key. "I want you to deliver something to her."

I was uncertain. The meeting already seemed to be over, but I did not know what I was supposed to do. "What would you like me to deliver, sir?" I asked.

Kessler sighed. He gestured delicately with his hands, as if he might not have the dexterity to explain the situation. "Marriage means very different things to different people," he began. "No matter what the varying state of it may be from one couple to the next, there are always certain allowances made. From one person to another. These . . . these allowances cannot go unreciprocated. . . ."

I paused inexpertly. Kessler touched his tie lightly, feathered his hair, and finally spoke again. "I want you to go deliver what's needed."

The room stood still. Was I hearing this? Many things I had heard since coming here were unorthodox, but this seemed completely odd. Kessler waited serenely while I puzzled out the situation. I was supposed to go to his wife. In return he enjoyed certain liberties.

"Look, kid, I know it sounds off. You feel like you're being set up. But if I wanted to set you up, you'd never see it coming. I'm just offering you an opportunity." Unsure of what to do, I knew I had to get out of there. I clasped the key in my fist and stood up, nodding, and went for the door. As I got into the freer air of the hall I could hear Kessler chuckle slightly and then yell at his assistant, "Get me somebody on the phone!"

As I drove toward the L'Ermitage, rivulets of sweat ran down my temples. Did I have a price? Was this it? It seemed I suddenly had so many questions about my own integrity that I needed to think over before answering. . . . I expected that these situations might come up, but I thought I wouldn't be encountering them for quite some time, that when I did I'd be more ready. I had commended myself for my firm grasp of my sexual identity, but was this what it gained me? Intellectually I could compete with those who had the jobs I wanted, yet here I was, fumbling like an inexperienced kid. Maybe I really wasn't ready yet. When it came to my possessing the intangibles that contributed to success, I suddenly had a hollow feeling in my stomach. I went through the lobby of the hotel in a daze and took the elevator to the top floor.

Walking down the plush-carpeted corridor, I found myself admiring the fine artwork on the walls. My mind would not focus on the situation, the task at hand, so to speak. I stopped, wondering at how the oil paintings were not stolen. I touched one and noticed it was bolted to the wall. I seemed to forget why I was there for a moment. I was not ready. Instead of going to the room, I walked up a flight of stairs leading to the rooftop pool. The view was incredible. I felt like an eagle soaring above the city. The famed hills stretched out in front of me in a display of opulence. Luxurious houses dotted the greenery of the trees in pink and white puffs like a grand bouquet. All of it was there because of the movie business. I felt again how much *I* wanted to be a part of it. I wanted to own one of the houses, to live here and create movies. I wanted it all. Breathing deeply, I went back down to the room. A soft strain of classical music lilted through the harshly air-conditioned halls. I felt young. The town fed on stories and youth, I realized, revising my earlier opinion. I went to use the key, but could not make it fit the lock. Instead I knocked.

I had expected a frowzy older woman in a clinging, outdated nightgown for some reason, but Mrs. Kessler opened the door wearing a wide-legged white pant suit made of silky fabric, and stylish dark sunglasses that covered any imperfections her surgery-smooth face might have held. I knew little of women's fashion, but I recognized she wore Chanel. Her hair was bobbed smartly, and her jacket revealed cleavage that looked too soft but inviting nonetheless. "I'm from the agency," I began.

"Aren't you pretty?" she said. "Why didn't you use the key?"

CHAPTER TWO

I started on Mickey Kessler's desk the next Monday. No mention was made by him about the events of the past week, and I certainly wasn't going to be the one to bring them up. My sense of near defeat at the hands of the mailroom quickly vanished as I became what was known as a second assistant. My co-worker, the main assistant who was to show me the ropes, was a brown-eyed kid, who never seemed to be very well shaved, named Lawrence Feller. Lawrence was older and had seniority over me, but I was soon the one who served in the advisory role. Lawrence didn't know how to carry himself so that he might be well regarded. He was too kind-seeming and up-front, and had no sense of boundary between his job and personal harassment. The town, I quickly learned, recognized this kind of person, like a shark sensing a drop of blood in ten miles square of ocean. I was fortunate to have such a vivid example right in front of my face. Lawrence Feller was a piece of chum. And Kessler, at whose hand I was to learn the trade, had gained renown equal to that of whipping his chair for his browbeating of assistants. Kessler was touted as a master at this, and while erudition about deal making would have to wait, studying abuse firsthand would not. On Thursday morning of my first week, upon arriving at work, the agent remarked to Lawrence Feller, "I don't like that tie."

"I'm sorry," said Feller of the offending item, a blue polysateen blend adorned with clover leafs and lightning-bolt-type slashes. "It's the only one I have." I winced at the raw vulnerability Lawrence showed in the situation, but the few hundred after taxes that Feller's salary provided was hardly enough for beef and board and car in a town that demanded one. Instead of apologizing for his lack of silk neck hangers, he should have been indignant.

He had shown weakness, though, and moments later Mickey Kessler emerged from his office, crossed to Feller, jerked the boy forward by the offending necktie, and cut it off just below the knot with a gleaming pair of scissors. Reentering his glass-walled cocoon, Kessler laughed like a medieval tax collector after calling on the local innkeeper. Feller was stunned as he sat feeling his stubby half Windsor, and considered aloud the levels of redress he might have from physical to legal.

"I'll stab him in the heart with those fucking scissors . . . I'll go to personnel about this . . . I'll—I'll sue the shit out of him . . ." I looked on silently, knowing Lawrence wouldn't act on his own behalf.

"I mean, can you believe that, Nathan?" Lawrence asked, trying to ease the embarrassment of the situation for himself.

"Yeah, Lawrence, I can. I really can. Kessler's unsound," I finally answered, trying to let him out of it, though I was caught in the rocky middle ground between compassion and disgust. I realized my compassion was the equivalent of pity in this case, and that it was merely a different shade of disgust.

Walking down the hall soon after my new appointment, I crossed paths with Shelby Stark, the formerly teary-eyed agent. This time, however, her head was up and her shoulders, padded within her blazer, were squared. She didn't even recognize me. I stopped in front of her and said, "Good to see you again, Ms. Stark." I wondered if it was wise to be the reminder of her weak moment. "Nathan Pitch. We met once before in your office. I'm on Mickey Kessler's desk now." At this she lit up a little.

"Oh, yes. We met that day I was upset. My nutritionist said it was a wheat-intolerance thing. I don't have that problem anymore," she said in a cool manner.

"Of course."

"Kessler's desk, huh? Straight out of the mailroom. You must be a real charger. He have you reading any scripts?" she asked.

"No. Not yet," I said, and at her knowing glance felt I should add, "But it's only been a few weeks. I'm sure he will."

"Don't hold your breath. Here's the thing, though. If you're interested, I have a script that needs reading . . ." she said, and I was a stationary target.

"I'd love to. Unless you think Kessler wouldn't like it—"

"Oh, he wouldn't mind. People do this all the time. Pick up the script on the way out today. I need it written up by tomorrow, though," she said, biting her lip.

"What?"

"The report you'll write for me is called 'coverage.' I'll put a sample in with the script." She smiled. "And, Nathan, by the way, don't mention this to Kessler. That's also the way everybody does it."

That night by the bright, clear light of my desk lamp, I read the script and made my first attempt at coverage. The worst thing about it was writing a "log line," reducing the entire screenplay to one sentence. Once, I had read, when Tolstoy was asked what *Anna Karenina* was about, he had answered, "It's about *Anna Karenina*, the way I wrote it, from beginning to end." Had he been able to tell it differently, or shorter, or otherwise, he would have. I felt a little sacrilegious about what I was doing, but the script was a long way from Tolstoy. My log line read: A gumshoe, hired to find a senator's kidnapped daughter, instead discovers the plans to a time machine that a fanatical militia group plans to use to destroy the world, before the gumshoe manages to foil the group, find the girl, and save the world. Phew. After the log line there was a short synopsis and then comments on the piece.

The next day Stark was happy with the results, and the process continued. She began giving me projects regularly. I would write them up, and she would decide whether to try to sell them or dump them and their creators. Shelby got free work from me, while I learned something new, made one of the "connections" I'd heard were so valuable, and plugged into the script pipeline as a reader for the first time. Fresh in town, mine was an unjaded opinion. I had real enthusiasm when discussing the stories, and that was one of the first commodities that vanished after arrival here. More important, Shelby went on to read the scripts I had recommended, and she shared my opinion on several occasions, which meant I was *right*, and had *good taste*. She said I "seemed like a potential executive to her," which thrilled me to hear.

In Kessler's office Feller now wore ties markedly similar to the boss's, while I began to gain a sort of following of other assistants who had heard me expound on the relative merits of current scripts I should not have even known about. The people around me were generally impressed by anyone who knew nearly anything from an undisclosed source. Not knowing where information came from, instead of making it suspect, as in journalistic circles, only sealed its pedigree in my world. I also became quietly known for my precise imitation of Charles Calloway, the president of the agency. He was a powerful man in the industry who had a clipped, nearly monotone, stationary-lipped way of speaking, and was said to emit a sense of great calm and control even in moments of fierce pressure. Often when things around the shop were tense, I would entertain Feller and myself by buzzing an agent's private phone line and in my best Calloway say: "It's Charles. My office. *Immediamente.*" Within seconds we would see an agent burst out of his particular glass-walled crypt, regardless of who he or she was meeting with, and beat their feet to Calloway's, where they would, with embarrassment, try to unravel the situation.

• • •

Some weeks after the necktie-cutting incident, Kessler
came to work and took note of poor Feller again. This time
the detail was his watch, which was a shabby copy of a popular
Russian model. "Come with me," he said to Feller, who
blindly followed him to the men's room. The agent made Feller
hold his wrist out over the commode, and with the exact same
pair of scissors he had used on the tie, he clipped the band.
The watch landed with a plunk in the toilet bowl, and was
promptly flushed by the agent's foot. Kessler returned several
steps ahead of the pale and coldly sweating Feller, who wore
a look of horror on his face from seeing firsthand exactly how
little resistance there was inside himself.

Feller cursed impotently under his breath, angry little saliva
bubbles forming along his lips. I felt I must intervene, to at
least counsel my colleague, and so chose the moment and took
Lawrence aside.

"Feller," I said, "you're going to have to do something about
Mickey and his goddamn scissors."

"Sure, Pitch, and get fired," Lawrence responded.

"I'm not saying you take him to court, just tell him to back
off. No, tell him to fuck off. He'll love that kind of talk. They
all do around here. If you don't get yourself some respect, he's
gonna be cutting your heart out one day," I said, letting him
have it and liking the feeling.

"I don't want to be known as an attitude problem. You know
what that can do to a career. I want to be thought of as a team
guy. Then I'll move up and get my own team," Lawrence said
robustly. He was parroting the fallacious idea that power came

to everyone who stayed in town long enough. I had heard it before; everyone at the bottom was sure that one day they were going to be on top. No one considered the distinct lack of room up there.

"As long as you have a plan," I said, losing steam and not quite accepting that I had heard such foolish talk from the man.

" I want to make films!" Feller threw in, a little too loudly after me as I walked away, really convincing himself now.

You couldn't make noise, I thought, though I said nothing more.

It was about this time that Kessler's stock really went up in town, and as I placed his calls and listened to them in order to take notes and keep track of any follow-ups needed, I heard how. A star-studded dirigible was being cast by one studio, and Kessler got the part of a judge for a classic old character actor whose career had been quiet for a few years. Phoning to tell him the news, Mickey spoke with his wife.

"It's Mickey Kessler, I've got to talk to him. I've got news," he began.

"I doubt very much if it'd interest him, Mr. Kessler," the old lady replied.

"You let me talk to him, we'll see who's interested," Kessler continued excitedly.

"He died a year and a half ago, Mr. Kessler. You sent flowers."

"I did?" Kessler blanched. "I'm very sorry." Hanging up the receiver but keeping the instrument in his hand, he opened his mouth and yelled one word: "Feller!"

Lawrence darted into the office as I looked on. Kessler hurled the phone at him, missing high and right, smashing it and taking out a piece of acoustical ceiling tile with it.

"Goddamn you, Feller, did you know I just booked a dead client?"

"No, sir. I swear. What should I do?" Lawrence fumbled.

"TAKE. HUME. SANDERS. OFF. THE. ROLODEX," Kessler barked, pronouncing what could only be defined as the terminal state in town. For me it explained quite a bit. One could be dead but still on the Rolodex, and therefore not forgotten, still in play. One could be alive and off the Rolodex, which was something apparently worse than death. But only after one was dead *and* off the Rolodex was one's fate truly decided and soul gone to rest. Feller, finally starting to wise up, got out of Mickey's way, leaving me to handle the phones alone, and allowing me to watch the man work even more closely. Kessler picked up his bullwhip and slowly uncurled it, using a gentle counter-clockwise twist of the wrist. The ravaged chair shuddered under the crack of the lash as I hurriedly replaced Kessler's phone, conferenced Kessler with the producer and casting director of the film in which he had gotten Hume Sanders, R.I.P., a role.

"Marty," Kessler began, "we've got to talk about Hume Sanders' price."

"I thought we settled this at dinner last night," the producer attempted.

Kessler charmed him. "Great dinner, no?"

"We'll go his last quote. Plus ten," the producer said.

"Ten?" Mickey baited.

"Plus twenty-five," the producer offered.

"I don't know if I can give you him for that," Mickey countered. "This is Hume Sanders we're talking about."

"Listen, Mickey, I love Hume Sanders, you know that," the casting director interjected, "but word is he's not doing too well."

"When has Hume Sanders failed to deliver?" Kessler asked.

"The man *is* a professional. From the old school," the producer said, suddenly siding with Mickey, it seemed, not wanting to offend. "Okay . . . We'll double his quote."

"Think of his body of work. Think of his class. He's underexposed. He's well rested," Kessler pressed. "I can't embarrass him with that number."

"You know . . . he is perfect for this project," the casting director allowed, while the producer weighed the idea.

"Double his quote. Plus twenty-five. I can't go a penny higher," the producer said with finality.

"Look, guys, I know how much Hume wants to do the part, but I have to get Charles Calloway to sign off on this, and I know he has his heart set on triple quote for this."

"Shit," the producer and the casting director breathed collectively. They knew that Charles Calloway was all powerful in these and many other matters, and as a result, completely inflexible.

"Guys. I'm wearing two hats on this one. I'm Hume's agent, but I'm working for you too, because even though I'm on the business end, I still consider myself a filmmaker." I almost laughed aloud at this and kept my finger firmly on the mute button of my phone. "I'll do what I can to sell Calloway on this." Mickey hung up and leaned back with a smile. Later that afternoon he simply called back and said Calloway had declined the offer. Mickey then went about spreading the story for the rest of the afternoon of how he had booked a dead client and tripled his quote. The feat solidified his place in the business. He became nearly untouchable in town.

One night the next month, as a reward for all my script reading, I received a dinner invitation to the home of Shelby Stark and her husband, Don. Their house was tucked away in the hills north of the university. I rang their doorbell, a bottle of inexpensive chablis, condensation bleeding through its paper sack, clutched in my hands. I was led inside by Shelby, who was casually dressed. She wore black leggings and a clinging mini T-shirt. Her dirty blond hair rose above her head like a fountain, held in place by a terry-cloth donut. She gave me an aggressive hug right there in the foyer that enabled me to feel her sinewy body through her thin clothing. So unprepared was I for this that the neck of the chablis angled between us and jabbed her beneath the ribs, causing her hand to go to the spot as she backed away.

"It's great to see you, Nathan," she said breathily, "I'm so glad we could become *friends* outside the office."

She showed me into the dining room, where her husband sat at the table. Don was in his mid-thirties but had gone prematurely and totally gray. He was bent over a disassembled piece of electronics consisting of a small box, wires, and tiny earpiece.

"How are you," he said upon our introduction, looking up at me with flat, tired eyes before going back to his work.

"Put that thing away, we have company," Shelby dictated with a voice heated by annoyance. His hands obeyed and pushed the equipment to the side, and he straightened in his chair. Shelby left the room to see about the dinner, and I perched myself uncomfortably on a fancy chair. Mr. Stark addressed my questioning gaze.

"It's a Vo-Ax 4100. . . ." This did not clarify things for me. "It's a sound-amplification device," he elaborated. I thought, perhaps, he was hard of hearing. "For picking up conversations across the room. . . . My line of work, I need information any way I can get it. . . ." The skin around his eyes pinched in spider webs of wrinkles. He looked haunted and beleaguered.

What line of work is that? I wondered as I took in their dining room, which was dominated by an armoire. The large cherrywood piece had shelves lined with what I took for an antique green bottle collection. The empty bottles bore unfamiliar marcasite labels embossed with silver leaves on winding vines.

"He's in development," Shelby informed me, entering with a platter of seared salmon and sautéed kale. At first I pictured this pale wisp of a husband in a drive-up photo booth, or in a lab working on the actual exposure of negatives, but of course he was an executive at a production company.

"Vice president," he informed me. What the man did was read projects, pass them on to his boss, a movie producer, who made the decisions on whether or not to buy them. If they were purchased, Mr. Stark would write notes for the screen-writers to follow in their rewrites in order to make the project ready for production. Apparently these development people knew better how to finish something than the writers, and when it came to the actual production of the films, that was someone else's job altogether. As I tucked into my nearly raw fish, I admired them as a couple, and admired myself for being in their company. He was the first non-agency executive I had socialized with, and I had parlayed my relationship with her to outside the office. My father would be proud.

Stark swore by the sound-enhancing device he'd been working on, said it yielded him project after project. He was able to hear agents discussing scripts and to begin soliciting them before his competitors knew of them. As he talked about it, I considered development. It seemed that here was a more ideal area for me than agenting. I had opinions. Who didn't? I had no experience in the actualities of production. Development was theoretical. It could be perfect. I became restless.

"The thing I ask of my writers is that they give me something true, and from that uncover something magical. And I expect them to hit the act breaks on page thirty and ninety while they do it," Mr. Stark said. I felt unable to sit still and listen to their shop talk, thinking about my possible future as an idea man, a development executive. I looked up to see Shelby, sitting across from me, running a piece of pink salmon along her moist bottom lip and staring at me.

Uncomfortable, I excused myself to use their bathroom.

I closed the door behind me and noticed that on top of the toilet tank was a leather-bound diary. I looked at it for only a brief moment, knowing full well I could not resist. I picked it up and turned to the first page and read a short entry. It said: "Jan. 1st. Resolution: Please God, give me the strength to make love to my wife this year." That was enough. A chill went through me as I read it. I closed the book, put it back in its place, and considered what could have driven Stark to this statement. Whether it was the combination of his and his wife's personalities, or their careers, or if this was where one ended up when married to an agent. It seemed to confirm what I had been thinking about getting out of the agency and segueing into development. I washed my hands and eased open the door in time to hear a broken, muted accusation, "drool over . . . guest . . ." from Mr. Stark and a stony silence from Shelby in return. I returned to my meal and wordlessly picked over the kiwi meringue sorbet dessert. The tension between husband and wife didn't grow or diminish, but merely sat there like a fourth party at the dinner. I left as quickly as possible.

Over the next several days a strange, trapped feeling settled over me as I considered how I could inquire into and make the jump over to the creative side of the business. My days at the agency had become a blur, a high-pressure one, punctuated by Kessler's abuses of Feller. After the hundredth instance of Kessler smacking him in the back of the head with a script, Feller slunk out of the agent's office to our desk area. I shook my head, and Feller glared at me. "What do you want from me? I *need* this job. . . ." he nearly cried. It seemed everything I witnessed at work confirmed my desire to leave, that the whole agency side of the business was wrong for me.

Maybe it was the strain of so many people keeping up different facades, or perhaps it was the contrast of representing creative talent—and the complete absence of the same in themselves—or perhaps it was just the "sell, sell, sell" nature of the job, but the agency seemed to be a place where humanity stopped and something else began. It was like a large, wild animal, stricken with a fever and operating outside the laws of nature. And *needing* the job was what made one vulnerable to it. There was a code of conduct here, but it was warped and stood apart from, and above, the country's legal system. There was not even such a notion as "honor amongst thieves," as in politics, in this place. Favor bartering and making a deal were all that mattered. The bottom line was the bottom line. I felt I was on a flume ride while the flow of the business gushed around me, fed by an unnaturally high number of stories, injected into the system like growth hormones via coverage. The daily work had to be carried on regardless of whether it meant staying until midnight or showing up at six in the morning, or both. It could grind one down, and I saw it happening in Feller, who had those deepening, darkening bags under his eyes, as much as I felt it happening in myself. Kessler was constantly pressured to produce more, and the pressure filtered down to Feller and me. Our office troika was like a test organism under stress, in which something would have to give.

One morning the exhausted Lawrence Feller and I watched Mickey Kessler arrive with a cylindrical package wrapped in brown paper. He leaned it against the wall in his office, and that is where it stayed for several hours. After returning from lunch, the agent beckoned Lawrence into his glass-walled office. The assistant complied with serf-like acquiescence. Kessler had a filing task for Feller, it seemed, one that had been improperly carried out at least once in the recent past by the hapless assistant. The agent picked up a large stack of heavy-stock manila folders from his desk and thrust them toward Lawrence. The sharp edge of one of the files slashed the web between thumb and forefinger of the assistant's doughy hand. Deep vermilion rushed forth from the cut, and the effect it had on Kessler was palpable. It served to electrify him. He breathed through his nose, his jowls rippling like gills. "You know what, Feller, I'm tired of this weakness of yours. You know how much shit *I* had to eat coming up in the training program? You've had it too easy," Kessler said. Feller was made to kneel on the floor, while the agent removed a walnut burled Beretta custom twelve-gauge shotgun from the wrapped package and pointed it at the young man's head.

I looked up from my work with concern at the scene. Through the glass I could not tell if the pump-action gun was real and functional, until I heard the distinctive sound of Kessler racking the weapon over the din of fax machines and computers. My question wasn't whether or not Kessler would pull the trigger, I knew he would do that, but rather, was there a shell in the gun? The general office activity slowed. Carter, Trudy, and others in the office looked on more or less abjectly, each deciding for themself whether there was going to be a mess or not. Feller knelt in the deep pile carpet and began an approach toward hyperventilation. I paused, recalling a time in the not-so-distant past when my decision to help would have been automatic, but I now occupied a place where every action was best considered for the result it might yield and how it might most benefit oneself. I pondered turning my chair away from the wall of glass and concentrating on my computer screen until things were resolved, but after another moment I sighed and reached for my phone. Instead of dialing 911, I pushed the numbers 43. Mickey Kessler's private line.

Through the glass I could see the agent react to the sound of the intercom buzzer. Flicking his head toward the desk, he seemed determined to stick to the fundamentals of keeping his eyes where his gun was pointed, but on the other hand, it could be Calloway on the line. Feller, for his part, was fully focused on the muzzle of the twelve-gauge, his pupils reaching the approximate size of the bore. After the phone gave another interminable buzz, Kessler snapped the gun to a position resembling port arms, then laid it across the desktop. He answered the call.

"Charles. My office," I said in my best Calloway.

"Ah. Charles. I'm in the middle of something . . . I could really use one more minute to wrap it up," Mickey said in what would have been an unheralded show of rebellion had it really been Calloway on the line.

I could see Kessler's right hand move to the pistol grip of the shotgun while he held the phone with his left, and I chanced it all, *"Immediamente!"*

Kessler slammed down the phone, released the shotgun, and strode briskly out of the office, nearly before I could put down my own receiver. He marched stiffly down the hall toward Calloway's quarters. Feller, still kneeling, gave me a look that was lost in the no-man's land between gratitude, relief, and disappointment. I signaled him to get up. He seemed to have forgotten he was on his knees. As Lawrence climbed to his feet, I walked into the office and picked up the gun. I worked the pump's action, fully expecting to eject a shell. But it was empty. A sick bluff. I leaned the gun against the desk, ready to head out, for Kessler could be returning any minute, having discovered the ruse.

"Empty," was all Feller could say, staring at the gun. Then we saw Kessler on his way back to the office, and something in Feller snapped. Screaming, he tore down the hall at full speed, past a dozen cublicles, and barreled toward the plate-glass window that overlooked a crowded boulevard. The tortured assistant didn't slow a hitch as he passed a bemused Kessler, and hit the glass, plummeting to the street two stories below. The floor's various workers fell into dead silence and gathered by the newly opened window. Warm, stagnant street air flowed upward over the group, mixing with our escaping conditioned office air. Kessler followed the scene, casually striding down the hall with an admirable calm. He shouldered into the growing crowd and shouted down to the writhing assistant, who had miraculously only broken his leg.

"Christ, Feller! You can't even do that right, can you?" And with this line Kessler installed himself in the pantheon of the town's true super-agents.

Following the incident, Kessler was moved—unofficially promoted, it was whispered in certain circles—to a corner office away from the street-side windows. I went with him, and maintained the running of the office on my own. All parties agreed that Feller would receive vacation pay while his leg set, and that any court proceedings would be forgone with the understanding he could return to work when he was ready. The worst part of it all for Kessler was Calloway's seizure of his shotgun, personally. As for me, the workload in the new office, especially with Shelby's scripts to read, had me frazzled, and left me no time to look for other jobs. I spent my nights reading, and writing coverage, painstaking coverage. I got familiar with what the word painstaking was all about. I was meticulous, detailed, and impeccably honest in my opinions. If anything would set me apart in this business, I believed, it was this.

It was also during this time that, without my knowledge, Shelby Stark began using my coverage in staff meetings rather than reading scripts for herself. It would have truly amused me to witness the birth of Shelby Stark's reputation as an insightful and straight-shooting script analyst. I would have been flattered and full of resentment all at once at the notion of her getting credit for my good work. But I was, if not blissfully so, at least completely unaware that as I became more and more snowed under by my workload, Shelby Stark was rising in the ranks. Only one person recognized a certain incongruity in a previously uninspired junior agent's sudden acquisition of a new skill, and this was the steely, flinty, thorny Mickey Kessler. Commenting expertly on unread screenplays had long been Kessler's strong suit, and sitting in staff meetings, he became aware that he was witnessing the birth of another master.

One day after a staff meeting, as they filed by my desk, Kessler confronted her. "Good point in the meeting, Stark," Kessler said. "I mean, where do you get this shit—'Despite a seemingly limited commercial market for this project, I think there's real sleeper potential here because of its deeply American quality of pathos,' " he continued. It was the exact phrase I'd used about a script based on a famous book whose rights were in the public domain that I had read for Shelby. He grabbed her elbow and demanded, "Who's doing your fucking work for you?" She didn't go for it, though; this lady was a comer. All she did was grin—over his shoulder at me—and walk away.

Four weeks later Feller returned. He hobbled in with a walking cast, and it seemed something behind his sickly smile was as broken as his leg, maybe permanently too. He re-shouldered his tasks as his health permitted. There was a problem, though, in the way Kessler's sense of mercy operated. While Feller was away, Kessler had come to rely on my no-nonsense approach. He found me more capable than Feller, and since I didn't give him as much room to abuse me as Feller had, there was more time for work. Because of this he had made me his main assistant and relegated Feller to second. Feller was not pleased. Indeed, when he saw his effects moved to a smaller desk, off to the side, away from the office, a tangible shift took place in his demeanor. A rod seemed to straighten his spine, and his eyes were those of a wild dog who'd been driven from the pack. I was unnerved by it, but I didn't have time to hold Feller's hand as my own were full with Kessler, and Shelby Stark and her new requests.

Along with the coverage Shelby got from me, she increasingly wanted more of my time. We would meet, have a coffee or a drink, and talk about the scripts I had written up for her so she would have a more personal grasp of the projects. One particular evening when we were at a ubiquitous chain caffeine store, Shelby reached across the table, grasped my wrist, and said, "Nathan, I just wish there was more 'you' in your coverage." I was confused as to the nature of the statement and more so by the hand on my wrist.

"It's usually the anonymity of the critic that lends credibility to the criticism," I said. This woman was married. I knew her husband. What modicum of charm I might have had, I'd kept out of the office.

"It's just that I'd like to know you better," she sighed.

"What's to know?" I said. "I'm pretty plain once you get to know me."

"No, Nathan, you're so wrong," she argued. "Just the other day Don was talking about you. Saying how much he'd like to see more of you. You have no idea . . ." She trailed off. Her sentiment was curious. Everywhere else I had lived, there were always plenty just like me, and many more effervescent and fun-loving. Here, though, I realized, it was normalcy that was unconventional. I was as average an ingredient that could be added to a stock like this, but every dish needs something basic to hold it together. "I'm suggesting we become intimate," she said coyly. "Don would love to watch."

I felt a jolt run through me when she finally made her proposition. Without saying no or yes, without betraying any of my intentions, I managed to carry the conversation along.

"Look, Shelby, a situation like this, there are some things I need to know, boundaries to be established, areas to be shaded in, before I could consider proceeding," I said.

"We, Don, and I, haven't been, um, conjugal in five years," she began. This year didn't look like it would be the one either, I thought, recalling the diary entry, unless God came through in a handsome way. "I've had an affair or three in the past . . ." She went on without difficulty about the latest with an actor-client whom she visited on location in England. That had been over two years ago, I calculated, remembering the particular film's release date. I couldn't flatter myself regarding her selectivity, however, as once the subject was broached, I felt wanton desire coming off her as palpably as the steam did her coffee.

"You know, I wouldn't mind some of my coverage reaching Charles Calloway directly," I smiled. "And he should learn I wrote it," I said, in an act designed as much to entertain myself as actually achieve something.

Shelby sat back and nodded smugly. "I figured this about you, Nathan. All of Kessler's boys are known to go to certain *lengths*. . . . All except that cretinous Feller, he wasn't asked," she finished, shivering at the thought of him.

I flashed on Kessler's wife and I in the chilled air of the L'Ermitage suite, the situation to which Shelby was referring. A situation I had previously thought confidential. I had felt like a sliced and sectioned half grapefruit in a silver bowl that day, sitting on the divan like so much room service. Mrs.

Kessler put a glass of white wine in my hand despite it being 10:30 A.M., and for a little while it seemed she was more interested in talking. She was a beautiful woman, but I'd had the bad fortune to be nervous, which made her laugh, which then showed the crinkling skin beneath her expensive makeup. It hadn't been the wrinkles that had frightened me, but the way they were so completely hidden, only to emerge in an unguarded moment. It made me wary to believe anything I was seeing. Just when I thought things would remain distant and cordial, she came over and sat next to me. Close. She pressed into me with her shoulder and put her hand on my thigh. The smell she gave off was sweet, too deeply fragrant. It reminded me of being at home many years ago, three days after Mother's Day. The flower bouquets had started to go bad. I wondered where my mother was at the moment. Out on her horse, riding the furrowed land around her house, perhaps. I imagined Mrs. Kessler would not have been pleased to know I was thinking of my mother while with her.

Mrs. Kessler spoke some foolishness into my ear, her breath sour wine. "Once a woman hits forty, there's almost nothing that can be done to satisfy her . . . but don't worry, I'm still a few years away yet," she whispered.

My mother seemed to ride by in front of my eyes. I could hardly fathom her being in this situation, uttering similar sentiments. I suppose my lack of response let Mrs. Kessler know I wasn't her guy. She saw this, and the intervening decades that separated her from her youth, and began to crumble. She cried into my lap a bit because I didn't want her, apologizing the whole time, and I thought it all a little theatrical. Straightening up and dabbing her eyes, where her makeup had not run a rillet, she said, "Don't worry. I'll tell Mickey you made me happy."

"Thank you," I answered.

"You did too. Just by sitting with me and listening. . . . You're new in town, aren't you?" she asked.

"Yes," I said.

"Well, we'll take a rain check on this, then. Maybe after you've been around for a while I won't seem so horrible," she said, opening the door for me, really making me feel for her, and causing me to wish I was two people so that one of me could do what she wanted while the other went away.

After my reluctance with Mrs. Kessler, I was surprised to see myself playing it this way in my little parley with Shelby. I knew that if I hadn't gone ahead with an elegant, sensual woman like Mrs. Kessler, I definitely would not with a brittle number like Shelby. But months had passed, and I had changed. I'd come to realize that there was a curriculum I needed to master, and this kind of thing was a mere introductory course. Shelby and I left the café. "So let's agree to agree later." She smiled hawkishly and kissed me on the cheek. I nodded and got in my car. Offers and counteroffers were on the table, and a deal set in motion. And if I'd learned one bit of actual business from Mickey Kessler besides how to discuss scripts I had not yet read and how to return calls when the other person was at lunch or gone for the day, it was this: nothing was ever put on the table unless it could lead to a closing. Everything in between was mere negotiation.

• • •

The day of the next staff meeting was very warm and topped by a gray, haze-filled sky. It was one of those days when the hills, just a few blocks away from the office, were invisible. Such days made me uneasy, as though I had been placed on the canvas of a watercolorist who washed over the landscape with his heavy brush. Some people thought that barometric pressure was responsible for tense moods on days like this. I considered the theory while looking across at Feller. He looked up at me and smiled. Before Kessler had gone off to the staff meeting, Feller had been in with him. It must have gone well, for a change, for here was Feller, grinning mildly, more amiable and pleased-seeming than he ever had been before his "accident."

Down the hall I could see into the glass-encased conference room. The agents were all assembled, and in a rare event, Charles Calloway was in attendence. As assistants flowed in and out with beverages and files, I could hear snippets of the usual rundown on client bookings, new clients, available hot properties, and gossip, and then talk turned to a recently received project that would either be sent around to producers, given directly to the studios, or packaged with acting and directing clients, depending on its strength.

"Has anybody read this yet?" I heard Charles Calloway say as a mailroom worker carried out two empty coffeepots. The question seemed to send a tremor through Shelby Stark. "Can anybody discuss it?" Calloway continued.

"I can, Charles—" Shelby volunteered, beaming, before being cut off by the closing door. The next words I heard, as the door was swung open again and a breakfast cart was wheeled in, were spoken by Kessler.

". . . really, Stark, we all know where you're getting your scripts read," he said, a smug smile forming on his lips. My lungs froze and my ears expanded like radar dishes. The breakfast cart got wedged in the door, and the conversation flowed toward me as a mail roomer tried to free it.

"What are you talking about?" Shelby said. I guessed that she was intending to speak to Calloway about me, but not like this. There was no telling how he'd react.

"She's not going through regular channels for her story work, Charles," Kessler sang out nimbly. "She's got my assistant, Nathan Pitch, working for her. He's probably slipping it to her—" The room fell silent and heads swiveled between the participants in the conversation and then craned to look at me. There was a pregnant moment in which no one was sure what Calloway's response would be. Then he spoke.

"Mickey. You putz. I don't care where she gets her coverage," Calloway said, in his clipped, quiet way, shutting down Kessler and his little game. Seeing Kessler boxed away like so, Shelby smiled at first, as did I. Then I realized the dual truth of Calloway's statement. He didn't care who was writing the coverage, he just expected it. Therefore her doing me a favor was pretty much nullified, and my doing her the return service was going to be as well. The breakfast cart was freed, the door closed, and the meeting went on for an excruciating twenty more minutes.

As the meeting broke and agents rushed out to spread the

new gossip they'd heard, Shelby left the conference room tight-lipped and grim. She was just steps ahead of the grim and tight-lipped Mickey Kessler. They both headed toward Kessler's office and me. Feeling Mickey behind her, Shelby tried to nod casually at me sitting behind my desk, but was then forced to walk on. Kessler strode savagely by me, screaming my name, beckoning me into his office. He didn't so much as pause, kicking the door shut behind me, picking up his whip and lashing the chair with a vicious shot.

"You son of a bitch. You write coverage for that slut Shelby Stark and don't tell me about it?" he foamed.

"The only reason I did was because she showed me how," I answered. I considered knocking the whip out of his grasp and handing him a lesson, but then I considered his power in town and decided it would be career suicide.

"I didn't even know you were reading fucking scripts," Kessler spat, delivering another curling shot to the chair. This wasn't just regular anger; this was "agent caught out of the loop" rage. He had been impotent on this one, in his primary area of operation: information.

"You never gave me the chance," I retorted.

"I only *give* one opportunity; any others have to be ripped out of my hands. You made me look bad in front of Calloway."

"For doing extra work?"

"And don't try going to him about this either, I don't think he'd appreciate your impersonation." Kessler couldn't help himself; he looked out through the glass at Feller, his informant. My colleague, gazing on with interest, scurried after some paperwork upon being noticed. I had a new appreciation for the thorough schooling Feller was gaining in the training program.

"Son of a bitch," escaped my lips.

"You're fired," Kessler said, finally feeling back in control.

"You're firing me over this?" I asked, already relieved not to be working there.

"Not for this. For fucking my wife!" Kessler replied.

CHAPTER THREE

Axed. Let go. Shit-canned. How distinctly un-Warren Buffett-like. After Kessler's last statement I gathered my personals—a sweater that cut the chill of air-conditioning that was subarctic some days, a computer disk, and a book called the *Creative Directory* that listed all the companies and personnel in the production and development side of the business and headed for the exit. Shelby Stark caught me by the elevator, biting her lip in a way that left me wondering for whom, exactly, she was upset.

"That bastard," she said. "We'll get you a job at another agency. My friend from college—"

"Forget agencies. You can have 'em," I said, stepping into the elevator.

"We'll get you into development, then. Call me Monday. My husband can help you—" This last bit caused me to jab the Close Door button repeatedly and ride away.

Leaving the office on foot, I started to feel better immediately. Really, what I had noticed right away, on the elevator ride down, was that I was simply starting to feel again. Taking my first few steps into the sunlight, it seemed even the day was going to cooperate. The oppressive haze, optimistically called the *marine layer* by weathermen, had started to lift and dilute along with my mood. I decided I would wait before getting my car, walk around a bit, and revel in this newly awakened sentience. I discarded my sweater, an old favorite, with hardly a thought, and checked the bag holding my Rolodex and *Creative Directory* at a store. I began to feel a looseness flow throughout my limbs and especially my neck. By the time I'd gone a few blocks, I was aware of an all-over tingling as I jangled along.

"I'm not really walking," I quickly decided. "Walking is a gait fit for employed people . . . I'm ambling."

"What are you doing?" I imagined a passerby asking me.

"I'm out for an amble," I would answer. "This ambling has quite a salutary effect on one's constitution," I noted. "I wonder why I haven't done more of this in the past."

Only a few things might have added to my new mood: having quit flat-out before being fired, and having had another job lined up.

"No," I quickly decided, "had I quit, I would have felt so good I'd be walking on air now. Or dancing in the streets. I'd be elated, and that would throw off my ambling."

"Yes," I concluded, satisfied with my thinking, "a good dose of misfortune, gamely faced by the ambler, is largely responsible for the state."

I expected to feel the cloud of failure hanging over me at my termination. It was against the great American way to be booted like that. I did not feel failure, though, not right away. Rather, I felt helped by circumstance toward my true destination. The first sign that I was in the wrong place at the agency should have been looking around and not seeing anyone I admired there, but now it no longer mattered because I was free.

"To amble," I thought. The verb was my friend, and I appreciated it being along with me, for otherwise the day might have become a lonely one. I went up the pretty streets and down the well-kept alleys of Beverly Hills. I looked at the plush hotels, imagined being picked up there by limousine and whisked away to motion picture award ceremonies. I looked in the store windows at things I could not, and would not in the recognizable future, be able to afford. There were electronic gadget stores that featured robotic drink-serving butlers, chairs that kneaded the spine, vibrating pads that massaged the feet, and personal laser beams the size of a key chain. I passed galleries full of strange, colorful paintings and modern sculptures, more stores packed with more highly technical and marginally useful gadgets, boutiques which offered sumptuously textured but ghastly fashions, display cases ablaze with priceless gaudy jewelry, and salons that were both posh and forbidding. I was happy to report to myself that I had little use for it all anyway. Besides, I was ambling, and how, I wondered, could one buy and tote purchases and still amble properly?

No, right now I was embracing this one thing, and was

devoted to doing it expertly. "Boy," I thought, "I could sure give everyone at the agency a lesson in *focus*. In *application*." Lack of singular focus was a key reason the agency was such a troubled place. It was the division of energies, the splintering of concentration, that had them all going in eleven directions at once. Chasing a script with one hand, a client with the other, a new job with a third, a different project with yet another, it left them no choice but to be grossly underhanded. Had they all possesed the foresight, the insight, the Zen-like wisdom to zero in on one thing that I had and gave to them as example by way of my hundred percent concentrated ambling, then maybe they wouldn't be in the state they're in.

I used the word as much as I could in as many sentences and conjugations as I could. "I amble. I have ambled. I will be ambling again. I amble, therefore I am. . . ."

But no one has time for Zen in this town, and my thoughts turned to that other thing which would have made this day a better one—another job. I had some money, but it wouldn't last long. Asking my father was not an option. Sure, I didn't have many expenses, but food and rent had their own meter— and even the cracker box wasn't free. I also had no prospects for new work. I knew several people in the industry now, but how much help could I count on from them? No word other than *little* came to mind. All this thinking, and the fact that I had done something, done it well, but had done it to completion, slowed my step and turned my ambling back into walking.

"I'm trudging now," I realized, and that is not nearly as much fun. Heading back toward the agency to get my car, I collected my bag and made another stop—at a liquor store. I had, after all, been fired, and wasn't one supposed to get tanked on the occasion?

Although I knew I was supposed to get liquor, I had previously drank only in high school and collegiate celebration and had no idea what type was appropriate for getting in the bag on the day of a good sacking. I walked up and down the aisles deciding. I picked up a twelve-pack of beer, but no, it seemed too festive, more suited to a sporting event, outdoor concert, or date rape. I considered a bottle of vodka—but again it seemed to better fit girls away at the beach for the weekend with fruit juice mixers. Ouzo, grappa, anisette, all conjured up mandolins, good meals and breaking plates, and *tuaca*, what the hell was that? Scotch wasn't it, I hadn't suffered a stock market collapse. Whiskey struck me as the right choice, but I wasn't a bitter, burned-out cop. That's what they drank, I knew from all the screenplays I'd read. Finally, I grabbed a bottle of gin and, in a moment of insecurity, two bottles of wine. One white, one red. It might have been overkill, but I didn't have to drink it all. I took the sack, went to my car, and drove to the apartment.

Upon arrival at the cracker box, and my nemesis, the steady, unblinking answering machine light, I dropped my belongings and opened the bottle of red. It was a cheap, weak vintage cabernet more suitable for salad dressing than drinking. I poured myself a large glass. "Where to work?" I wondered, thumbing through some recent trades to the classifieds and drinking the wine in great gulps. I found there wasn't much besides secretarial offered in the trades, as the wine brought warm fatigue to my limbs. All the real jobs were passed along the grapevine, each bit of information carrying a price. I knew this, but had to check the papers to be sure.

I was halfway through the bottle when I opened the *Times* to look for non-industry situations. A slight financial panic was being born in me, and I drank to stay ahead of it. My head was pounding as I circled assistant managerial positions at restaurants, disregarding the years of experience the jobs called for. If it was anything like the movie industry, I could just bluff by without experience, by virtue of having been to a restaurant, as most film executives' only qualification was having seen a movie. The business had been perfect for me— young, possessing no impressive background, wafer-thin résumé, no skills. I had come here, where it didn't matter, where one could rise with or without any real reason save outlandish self-confidence and a fully self-confessed grasp of the marketplace. Conversely, people from other fields, advertising executives, lawyers, stockbrokers, would sometimes switch to the industry mid-career, willing to start at the bottom, believing that nothing they had learned previously had prepared them for the field. I was drunk by the time I arrived at the travel agency jobs. I hurled the empty wine bottle across the room into the kitchen sink, where it landed with a clunk that miffed me, since I had wanted the satisfaction of hearing it shatter. I accidentally bumped the coffee table with my knee, spilling the remainder of my glass, and decided it was time to either open the gin or go to bed.

Upon my first swallow of gin, I expected a refreshing sensation. I anticipated the soft, clean outlook that I'd heard many career drunks got from gin. I suppose I expected the onset of some wry British archness. Instead it burned, like hot berries and flowers in my throat, a taste I would have in my mouth for days. Fairly collapsing on the bed after a few long pulls, I cursed myself for my own obviousness. To get fired and then sauced, the height of the banal. I thought of just how much of my life had given way to the obvious and the superficial. I was being conditioned by bad art and an anemic life. After such a strong and steady diet of poor images, and scripts and books that were less than literature, it was already becoming nearly impossible to register a real achievement. When I saw a film or read something truly worthy now, my faculties were not fully prepared for it, and it came off as a flat or uncomfortable experience. With any work that was well done, it might take two or three times through the piece in order to fully appreciate it. And I didn't have that kind of time. No one did. I was being convinced by imposters. An overblown television story beat a dark, sublime character study for the best picture award, although looking back, the loser is later considered the best picture of the decade. . . . My thinking had reached a dead end, so I set my alarm early in order to give myself a full day's worth of employment seeking. I finally slunk off to a sleep plagued by cartoonish dreams of cannibals, dancing to the sound of drums, around a kettle with me in it. They sharpened their knives and prepared to cut my flesh into little cubes.

The first day after my soaker, I did manage to wake up early, though I felt that my head had been cored by an expensive multipurpose vegetable cutter sold in one of the fancy gadget stores. Following a dispiriting morning job hunt that consisted of typing tests and lies about my shorthand ability at a few of the studios, I gave up and went to a park where I fell asleep in the grass. Awakening with a brain ache from my poorly oxygenated blood and singed by the sun, I vowed not to drink like that again. My insides felt raw and looted, and besides, for the questions I had, gin could not provide answers. I thought of calling Shelby immediately, but decided it would be a weak and, if she turned on me, potentially disastrous move. Better to let the smoke clear, retrain my instruments, and then call, if not out of a position of strength, at least from one of autonomy. I was tested immediately in this, for upon returning home, my goading answering machine light blinked briskly three times, over and over. It was Shelby, imploring me with more or less urgency and innuendo to call so she could give me assistance. I checked the urge, finally erasing the messages. I had promised myself I wouldn't call and it was a time when keeping promises to myself mattered.

What followed was not an immediate recovery and a new, more satisfying job, though. Rather, I slogged through interviews for positions in unrelated fields, watched my money dwindle, and could not quite pull down even an assistant managerial position in a restaurant. I took up a series of unremarkable jobs. I worked as a waiter, poured at a local bar, folded at a clothing store, hammered in furniture repair, even dialed at a stock brokerage for about five minutes. It had been only two months since I'd left the agency, but it felt like years, and it was another month still before I would allow myself to call Shelby.

Finally, after the interminable four weeks, I did it. Home in cracker box central after work at my latest gig, telemarketing, I picked up the phone for the thousandth time that day, knowing she would be in the office working late. The receiver, pressing warmly against my chafed ear, brought on the urge to hang up, unplug the phone, and put it away in a box forever. Despite this I dialed like an automaton, then gritted my teeth at the idea she wouldn't take my call. After a short wait, though, there she was, same as ever. "So the rumors of your demise have been greatly exaggerated," she began.

"Hello, Shelby," I answered. "How did you manage in the fallout?"

"What fallout?" she trilled, and I discovered that whatever proportions the incident had taken on for me, it was business as usual for everyone else. My already red ears burned brighter as I realized this whole self-imposed exile was unnecessary. It would have been expected, the obvious thing, to have called her and everybody else involved, right after the episode, to enlist their help in finding new work. I was taking things personally in a business that took no notice of persons. I had indulged foolish pride in the pain of my situation, my isolation, and was stubborn about not being relieved of it easily.

"What've you been up to?" she asked.

"Reading the classics, studying the Flemish school down at the museum, learning archery—"

"I meant, where have you been working, wise ass."

"Sales. Over the phone," I answered, feeling doubly foolish.

"Oh, Nathan, what a waste. I'll call you right back," she said, and without a pause hung up. I was left wondering at the tone of her voice. Whether it was disappointment or just brusqueness, I could not tell. Perhaps she was embarrassed at our previous arrangement upon seeing my inability to find new work. I prepared myself for the brush-off. Moments later the phone rang and it was her. She had called a friend and lined up something for me. I would still have to interview, but it was a walk-through. A done deal. I would be working for a marketing company which conducted the research that predicted profits on a particular film. She went on, saying something about "focus groups." It hardly mattered. Just like that, and I was back in the game. This Shelby, she could make things happen. She navigated the business world admirably, working her blend of coy utility and attempted seduction. She had actually made a single phone call and gotten a job for me. And the months on my own had all but extinguished any caution with which I might regard the price of a favor.

I had my interview with a large black woman named Carol, who was friendly and down home with me although we had only just met. "You'll do fine if you're a people person, sugar," she said. I suspected she wasn't from the South at all, but affecting a manner. It was her thing. She was also a close friend of Shelby's, so we spent most of our time talking about her, yet Carol didn't quite recall her development-executive husband's name. I wondered how much Carol knew about me, and my past entanglement with Shelby, as she went on to describe the job.

"You'll be be assigned a soon-to-be-released movie that's to be 'test-screened.' You'll circulate through demographically different areas of the city and enlist people, people who ain't involved in the industry—the *great unwashed*, we call 'em—to come to the free showing. Afterward, we hand out questionnaires to the audience so they can comment on the film." She went on detailing questions that ranged from favorite moments to pacing to grading the actors' performances, and most important, if they would recommend the film to others. We then would enter the results into a database, and I would learn how to break down the audience results for the studio's marketing team. Right after the screenings we would run focus groups—twenty randomly selected audience members we would lead in a tape-recorded discussion about the film. A paltry salary would be my compensation. I wished I had some other, better opportunity than this, but I didn't. I found I was wishing a lot of things lately. Carol gave me a clipboard full of information and sign-up sheets, and told me where to report the next day, and that was that.

By the end of my first day out amongst the general paying audience, I was already thinking of the ways in which I could parlay my situation into a mainline development job. After a few weeks of it, I was trying even harder. This was due to the fact that my simple job was actually very difficult. As I pounded the pavement all over the city, finally in contact with the thing that made movies so valuable—the audience—I found that I could barely find enough interested people to attend screenings who weren't already working in the industry. I came to believe that if there was indeed a great unwashed, it must be located somewhere else.

"Would you like to see a free screening?" I would ask.

"Who's in it?" would be the natural response.

"Alan Asher," I might say.

"Don't like him," might be the answer.

If I got a "Yes, I'd love to," I would then continue, "May I ask your occupation?"

"I'm a gaffer," or "key grip," "cameraman," "sound editor," "agent," "actor," "script supervisor," and I would have to tell them they weren't eligible. Often I would begin my rap and the person would cut me off, knowing the drill and saying he or she was in the business. Hearing this so often, I was left with the desire to shake them and implore, "Where? Where do you work? How about a job?" I did ask one young lady if there were any openings at her company, only to see her scurry away as if I had told her I had a serious airborne virus. I spent all day talking to passersby and finally, finally when I'd get one who was "non-pro," as it was called, when I had gone through the whole process and they said they weren't in the industry and they'd like to attend, I had the urge to throw my arms around them, hug them for coming along and filling up one of the seats it was my responsibility to get rid of.

If I was not going to meet industry people with whom I could network while out in the streets, and the screenings were limited to outsiders, then the data-input sessions amongst my co-workers were even more dispiriting, for they meant time spent with others merely stuck in the same situation as me. No one I worked with was making a career of the marketing company, it seemed, except for Carol. The place was just a way station. Everybody was en route to a different arm of the business. We were really a bunch of people making careers of looking for careers.

My first month and then my second wore on, and my knowledge of audience questionnaires deepened. I spent far more time than the job required poring over the response sheets, gleaning from them information about the audiences. I began to be able to tell without checking, based solely on their comments, what age the respondents were, and from what segment of society, whether or not they liked their jobs, if they could stand their spouse, and what their political affiliation was. I saw how a light comedy tested like bad sex. People there solely for the event liked the experience, but it wasn't something they would go out of their way to pay for. This caused fits for the studios, since these films promised a profit when screened for free, but would bomb in the marketplace when a paying audience did not show up. I felt knowing the taste of the masses was the one useful tool I could take away from this job.

My focus group patter also deepened beyond the rote to the ingrained. "Thank you all so much for staying on after the film. As you know, this is one of the very first screenings of the film, and your comments are very important to the filmmakers. I have nothing to do with the making of the film, so please be as honest as possible, and please speak loudly for the tape recorders. The session will not be recorded for radio or television, so don't worry about that. It's only to help with my own notes. . . ." I would then lead the group through questions and watch as each group member puffed up with importance and took on the role of film critic for a day. And important they were. Pauline Kael and her ilk, scribbling earnestly after the fact, never wrote a review that had as much impact as when a certain number of these audience respondents agreed on a point. If an overwhelming amount of comments suggested a change in a film, especially a different ending, the studios would go back and reshoot it that way before release. Whatever the writers, directors, and producers had originally intended was no longer considered important if those with the ticket money wanted to see something different. My test groups resurrected more characters than Jesus ever did. The actors would be shot up beyond recognition, as dead as Hoffa, at the end of the director's cut, only to come back, badly wounded but gamely hanging on in a new reel quickly thrown together before release. I learned a malignant fact while working in market research, and I learned it indelibly— that as a priority, storytelling was well behind counting money in this town, and it never was going to catch up.

Back in the office, filing my paperwork after a rough shift, I listened to the rest of the audience fillers. "Can you cover for me tomorrow?" one asked.

"Audition?" the other asked.

"Meeting with an agent."

"Casting, commercial, or talent?" someone else wondered.

"Commercial."

"You should meet mine, over at Penny Silver Associates."

"They get you work?" yet another queried.

"They landed me that chocolate milk commercial," said the worker.

"Who's your agent?" the first asked no one in particular.

"Oh, I left him. I'm going to graduate school in the fall," someone responded.

"I am too. I'm going to law school, so I can become an agent," a different one offered.

"I'm going to film school," the other said.

"You can direct us in your films, then," one of the actor hopefuls volunteered.

"Wouldn't it be great if in a couple of years we were all working together, but as actors and directors and agents? Doing what we want to do and really successful and everything," another one, a plump blonde from dairy country, said. The room went quiet. She must have been painfully new in town. Her dreaminess threw a somewhat embarrassed pall over the rest of us, who went back to work with a more frenetic but bitter sort of energy. Most of these people were several years older than I. Some had just arrived, switching from other fields; some had been around for many years. Watching them like this gave me the sneaking, fleeting impression of my good, vital, early twenties years being sucked away while I was off in pursuit of a serpentine dream. I was a bit overwhelmed and more than a trace saddened by what I saw, which was everyone here desiring and deserving the chance to stand out, to burn brightly across the sky, to have their lousy quarter. That was what the movies gave the audiences for a few hours, and it was what everyone inside the business wanted as well. That's why we were all here. As fast, though, as a few people could become rich, or famous, as quickly as heroes could rise up and move through the public eye and become the icons of these dreams, there were just too damn many of us out there in line. There was a near impossibility of achieving special-ness, and specialness was just what everybody wanted.

"At least we're going after what we want, not settling," was a constant refrain used amongst us, the struggling, to ward off word of our friends from our previous lives, as they rose to broker, vice president, partner, and more in their more con-ventional fields. But I had worked at the agency, and I had seen the résumés ignored, eight-by-tens discarded, the video-tapes thrown away without being viewed, the scripts recycled unread. I knew that somewhere nearby there was a stinking, smoldering, fly-buzzing landfill made up of ambition. And this led me to the part that I truly did not understand—how could I be witness to so much folly and yet have the same core of ambition smoldering in my guts? I understood percentages, so I knew that of the few hundred or more young people I had encountered at the agency and worked with here, perhaps one might achieve his or her dreams in this town. I also swore to myself that if there could be only one, it would be me.

One Thursday, several months into the job, after a day's worth of audience sign-ups and studying market research, I was in the theater awaiting the current audience for a new thriller we were testing. The crowd entered, some veterans ready to slog through yet another focus group, some new in town and brimming with excitement over the insider nature of the event, some just happy to have a place to go for a couple of hours. I thought, with chagrin, back to my own first days in town, when I believed I was to be responsible for a great film, one that would change people's lives. Along with mine, I felt scores of these dream corpses blowing about in the frigid air-conditioned theater. Just then I saw a familiar figure in a custom-tailored glen plaid suit make his way furtively down the aisle to a choice seat. I doubted my own eyes at my good fortune—it was Mickey Kessler, super agent.

I had witnessed the fate of several lower-profile agents, and some producers, who had been recognized as industry professionals at the screenings. Quite a few had been denied admittance. Some felt compelled to try to talk their way in, dropping influential names, in what turned out to be embarrassing and futile displays. A couple of agents had actually been caught inside on one occasion when the focus group organizer, along with several theater ushers, had escorted them out kicking and braying. The films we screened could often be acquired on videotape from the studios within days, but that did not stop agents from trying to attain the forbidden. And to see an agent denied something is to truly see that agent's interest in it come alive. I decided there must be a pressing reason for Kessler to be out amongst the heathen, and supposed the suspenseful nature of the night's film might have prompted the studio to limit its exposure. Regardless, this was a screening for non-industry people only, and here was one Mickey Kessler, fat cat, and I had him dead to rights.

Walking down the aisle toward him, I noted several ushers at various exits, and watched Kessler checking the time nervously. The agent was always on a tight schedule. I approached him from over his right shoulder, like a fighter wheeling out of the sun, and as I walked I considered the state of the average citizen in the entertainment business: if he didn't take his own actions seriously, then no one else could either. By simply immersing oneself in the town's fanciful workings, one could divorce oneself from previous actions, present attachments, and future responsibilities. I could do this too. Here and now I could be whoever I chose to be. I felt I had very little to lose.

"Would you like some popcorn, Kessler?" I asked, arriving in front of him.

"Pitch." Kessler nodded curtly.

"This is a non-industry screening, you know," I said as blandly as I could.

"That's why you're here, I suppose," he said in an insult-laced tone.

"No, actually, I work for the audience company. So I'm going to have to ask you to leave," I said evenly. I did not want to overplay things.

"I'm just here to see how an actress—a bit player—looks on screen. A potential client," Kessler said, unwilling to be pushed.

"You can't be here," I stated, maybe a bit rushed. I felt my heart thump.

"Look, Nathan, I just want to see how Elizabeth Morgan looks. If she can read a line. You know I could get tape on her with one phone call," Kessler intoned in a confident whine, secure that this would settle things.

"Go get it, then," I said with finality, raising my hand to signal an usher. I was half embarrassed that I would claim a victory so small as inconveniencing this man, but I would weigh that later. I could practically hear Kessler's thoughts. The agent considered an advance look at this movie as giving him the opportunity to get a young client. If she was good, it would all be worth it.

"I sense another opportunity might be on your mind?" Kessler offered tentatively. He shifted in his seat. How much easier this would be for him if he could just pull out his money clip and take care of me. But he sensed that I wasn't going that cheap. I just shrugged.

"Call Eddie Upland at Iceberg Productions. They need a low-level development guy. Use my name," Kessler offered.

"Enjoy the show," I said, walking up the aisle.

I felt the swell of knowing in me. I had learned a few things about how the machinery worked. The job in question was mine, and in a strange way I finally deserved it.

I was only a few feet gone when Kessler turned around and apparently couldn't resist shouting after me, "By the way, they made your buddy Feller a junior agent. Imagine that."

Still walking, I looked back. "Regards to your wife, Mickey." I smiled.

CHAPTER FOUR

I walked into the ultramodern Beverly Hills offices of Iceberg Productions and could immediately sense in the very air
that the place was more relaxed than the agency. The waiting
area was decorated with sleek leather couches and chairs, and
solid wooden end tables, while the walls were hung with
framed one-sheets of films which the company had produced.
They were high-concept pictures, the kind that could be explained in one sentence and made a lot of money. A secretary
nearby was busy but not maddeningly so. A coffee area and
a photocopy machine stood quiet, unlike the agency's phalanx
of machines, which operated like a submarine torpedo bay
during a battle. Music played from a hidden sound system.

I was shown into the office of Eddie Upland, the vice president of development, to whom I would report. Yet another
V.P. in a town full of them. I was seated on a hunter green
sofa while he reclined with a loafered, sockless foot slung over

the arm of a friendly leather desk chair without a single whip mark on it. The desk in front of him was covered with promotional items—figurines, bumper stickers, key chains, and dolls—from recently released movies, and the bookshelves behind him were exploding with scripts.

"So, I hear good things about you. . . ." Upland began. He had the voice and face of a boy, and only the vertical furrow between his eyes was that of an older, more weathered man.

"Thank you," I replied, wondering where he had heard it.

"And who sent you over? . . ." Upland said, feigning forgetfulness.

"Mickey Kessler."

"Right, Mickey. Great guy," he offered heartily. Upland wore a crisp, buttoned-down oxford shirt and sharply creased charcoal gray slacks, what I would come to know as his uniform.

"Yeah."

"How do you know Mickey?" he asked.

"Worked on his desk," I responded, curious to see how I would handle the subject of my own firing.

"Had enough of that agency stuff, huh?" he offered.

"I guess so," I answered.

"Ready to get involved in the creative end?"

"Absolutely."

As we continued with our chat, Upland asked me in a bluff and enthusiastic way what I had seen and liked lately. I offered some titles that he had also liked. That seemed to be all it took; once again I had good taste. I mentioned some books for good measure, a couple that had been adapted to the screen, a few that would make for interesting adaptations, one I was supposed to have read in high school. Upland spoke about the film versions, how they had worked or failed. He did not say anything about the books themselves. He talked about my title—director of development—and the nature of the job, the fact that I would be responsible for reading material, commenting on it, finding new material, and writing "creative notes" on projects that we had in development.

"I tried my hand at writing screenplays," Upland volunteered, "but it was too solitary. I wanted to work in an office. A more social environment. Now I make a suggestion—a scene or a line—to the writer, and it shows up in the next draft. Just like writing. Best of both worlds." So pleased was I to be newly employed, to be back on the tycoon trail, that I allowed myself to believe there was nothing suspect in his statement.

He scribbled a figure on a piece of paper and slid it across the desk toward me, apologizing at the modest nature of the salary and the fact that I wouldn't have my own assistant. Realizing that I would no longer *be* the assistant, answering phones and doing the most puerile of bidding for anybody other than myself, I wanted to burst into chants of joy, and then reading the number, which was more than I had been making at any of my other jobs, I generously reassured him that it wouldn't be a problem. That not only was I a self-starter but a self-maintainer as well.

As for the principal of the company, one well-known producer named Jumper Sussman, well, he wasn't around much, especially when we weren't in production, which had been the whole two years that Upland had been working here. On my way out he told me the boss could often be found shopping for new cars.

"They bring six, seven new models over to his house, let him pick over them, then drive away the ones he doesn't want—if there are any. . . ." Upland chuckled mirthlessly to himself. I left with a stack of scripts that the company had in active development and was currently either attempting to find independent financing for or, more desirably, place at a studio. I was to read them that weekend and write up my opinions in detail.

That night, and all through the weekend, I holed up in my apartment and sped through the projects, writing down my thoughts on them. I got into some of the new material as well, writing coverage on it for my first day on the job. I focused my powers of analysis and tried to cultivate my insight and ability to be candid. I had to be careful, though, to write the synopsis immediately after finishing each script, for moments later I would start to forget what, exactly, each was about. In fact, I couldn't trust myself, without double checking, to be sure of whether or not I was combining the story line of two or several scripts I'd just read or had read in the past. I tried not to take this as a bad sign.

Monday morning, before I went to my new office, I stopped and looked at myself in the mirror. My eyes were set deeper than I remembered, and I had a few new lines around my mouth. I appeared older than my years and thought back over the difficult months now behind me. I vowed to start fresh and unjaded at this new job, to make myself wide-eyed and open toward the business again. Barring the arrival of any revolutionary new ideas on finding the key to life, I decided I would cling, perhaps in vain, to my traditional ideas that working hard and succeeding at my job would lead to financial and personal reward. I would soon be able to talk proudly to my father again of progress and triumph in my chosen field. I felt it true that when one was working and getting paid, being moderately entertained and inspired by one's work, the world was a decent, unsurprising place. A place with potential. Even this town, with all the dank, strange byways I had already encountered, could be navigated by a noble and upright person who had the focus and the faith to take it on his own terms. "I am that person," I told my reflection. I would present myself in the workplace with pride but not ego, dignity yet humility. Sheer will, perseverance, and ability would help me rise above the shady players, and compensate for the shortcuts that they were taking and I was forgoing.

I showed up to work early that morning, styrofoam cup of espresso in hand, and was surprised to see that Upland's office was still dark, that he wasn't in yet. I entered the small area that was to be my work space, a sort of keyhole between Upland's office and a conference room, that nonetheless provided some privacy, and set a few of my things out on the desk. I took stock of the supplies I would need, and coming to the end of the task fairly quickly, with still no sign of Upland, I felt my blood go a little syrupy with panic as I realized that as far as my job went, I had no idea of what I was supposed to do. Unsure where to even start, I thumbed through a couple of screenplays that were lying around and tried to look occupied until Upland walked in eating a muffin.

"Hey, Nathan," he said, trailing crumbs behind him as he went into his office. "You have a breakfast today?"

"No. I ate at home," I said lamely.

"I figured you had a breakfast meeting, that's why you're in so early. I had two, that's why I'm late," Upland said, shoving the last of the muffin into his mouth in a shower of cake debris, and waving a banana at me. "Jaime Matan and Cary Fields, both good people to stay close with . . ." I nodded in agreement, although I did not know the people he had had his two breakfasts with, indeed didn't know if they were men or women. I studied Upland. He was just smooth enough to be a slick player, almost handsome enough to be an actor, and nearly gritty enough to look like a director. The two breakfasts, a muffin, and a banana were just a start on the executive's nonstop day of eating. Fruit and sandwiches and snacks and cookies all morning, a heavy power lunch, another sandwich in the afternoon, drinks and a fancy dinner meeting at night. Upland was constantly in feed mode, but it didn't show on him. It was as if none of the food really stuck, and eating it was just another process to be diligently gone through.

"You have a lunch scheduled today?" Upland asked.

"Yes," I lied, feeling it crucial. "Someone from the agency."

"Good. Can't be close enough with them either," Upland agreed. Then we sat down and spent most of the morning going over the status of each of the company's projects. They were all simplistic and relied on our landing big stars for the lead roles, and would probably be very popular if we did. There was *Mr. Backward*, a comedy, for instance. What if a man woke up on the day he died and started living his life in reverse? I gave potential casting ideas that were probably obvious but which Upland seemed to take to heart. My coverage work was also well received by him.

"Tonight I want you to come to a screening with me over at the Directors Guild. Meet some people," he said in reward, strapping on his headset to begin a message pad's worth of phone calls. I went back to my office and acted busy for a little while until Upland left for lunch. I then slipped out to an inconspicuous diner to create a story about the lunch meeting I was supposed to have been at. It turned out that Upland never asked. He returned from his own lunch at three-thirty and went right into his office for three hours before the screening.

Sitting in the plush and darkened auditorium, I finally felt all around me the closeness of the industry's soldiers. I had driven myself to the glass tube building that was home to the Directors Guild, and when I'd used the Iceberg company name and gained entrance, I felt the strongest sense of validation I'd had since arriving in town. The screenings that night were a showcase of short works of the university's best filmmaking graduate students. Tucked into my deep red velvet seat, I glanced around with anticipation at the loosely suited and sharply coiffed crowd. This was the real thing, almost like the focus screenings inverted. No one *outside* the industry was allowed in here. Every few seats an unruly head of hair or a baseball cap signaled the presence of a director, cinematographer, crew member, or other creative type, which only added to the authenticity of the scene for me. I was so looking forward, in fact, to the post-screening reception that I had to force myself to watch the films.

The films themselves were earnest, irreverent, and artistic pieces in turn, that when shown in sequence six in a row numbed me into submission. Although these were the résumés that gained directors their first studio directing assignments, I had a hard time believing that the twelve-minute pieces I was watching were all it took to get control of several million dollars of someone else's money. At last, when the pictures were finally over, the crowd filed out into a large anteroom for the ever popular "spread." It was just as I had imagined. There were service bars dispensing cocktails, and tuxedoed waiters carrying hors d'oeuvres. The madding crowd around me vied for tidbits from the food trays floating through the room, and as I listened, I caught the occasional hushed criticism of "this year's crop" and mostly heard very boisterous praises sung. Things moved like a carousel around me until I felt hot and dizzy.

Stepping out and off to the side for a breather and to better sight Upland, I found myself standing next to a disheveled and ghostly pale young man who kept his back to the crowd and gave the impression that he was looking for a door through which to escape in the wood grain of the wall paneling. As I peered into the melee and the man faced out, we made eye contact and smiled an insincere greeting to one another.

"Director?" I chanced. The man nodded.

"Are you in production?" he asked back.

"Development," I answered with a gusto I failed to mute. "Which film was yours?"

"Day at the Beach. It was my first," the nervous man answered.

"Oh, the best one," I said, trying to get with the spirit of the function with a grand compliment, feeling much like I was timing the jump onto a moving freight train. Whether or not the film had actually been the best one, I did not know, although it wasn't the worst. His was a strange sort of comedy that began with an idyllic shot of fun and frolic on a Malibu–type beach. After the long weekend of reading scripts it seemed my mind automatically formatted the film into screenplay terms:

FADE IN:
EXT. BEACH—DAY

A beach filled with SUNBATHERS, SURFERS, and bikini-clad BLONDES playing volleyball.

ANGLE ON: Three grizzled MEN arrive on the beach wearing yellow heavy-weather rain gear, black rubber thigh-high boots, and carrying large duffel bags.
They move down to water's edge and unpack a sturdy rubber boat from one of the bags, which they proceed to inflate.

Just as they screw together two large oars and make to shove off the shore, a loose volleyball rolls up to their feet.

> BLONDE
> A little help? . . .

One of the Men picks it up and tosses it back to the players.

                                                    CUT TO:

EXT. RUBBER BOAT—SAME

Two of the Men, each manning an oar, really put their backs into it and row through the breakers out into the open water.

The third Man unzips a case and screws together a mighty, modern harpoon, the sun glinting off its razor tip.

Locking the oars against the gunwhales, one of the men shouts, saliva flying . . .

> MAN (Shouts)
> Thar she blows . . .

The harpooneer lets fly and lands a direct hit to a large whale.

EXT. WHALE—SAME

Scene of harpooned whale is edited in with stock whaling footage.

EXT. RUBBER BOAT—LATER

The three Men reel in the huge mammal with a chorus of grunts, and sing a whaling chantey while they row back to shore with their leviathan prize in tow.

MEN
*Tech—ADR whaling chantey.

EXT. BEACH—LATER

Back on land, the heavily sweating men beach the whale
and, producing a large machete-type blade, open the
whale's belly. (Stock footage)
Blood and offal fly from it, splashing the whalers up
their hip boots.

ANGLE ON: Again the fluffy white volleyball rolls
their way.

BLONDE
Little help . . .

CLOSE-UP: One man reaches for it, this time defiling
the ball's purity with his bloody hand.

TWO SHOT: Yet again he tosses it back with a smile.
The three turn to each other in a hug, one shouting
exuberantly.

MAN (Shouts)
It doesn't get any better than this . . .

Crane shot of the beach pulling back, back, back into
the distance . . .

FADE OUT.

The film showed an odd sensibility, and from what I knew
from focus groups, middle America probably wasn't ready for
it. I had no idea how to continue the conversation with the
film's creator, and I felt an animosity between him and me

begin to grow out of thin air. To each of us the other's presence seemed the reason for our discomfort. I decided to go with the basics.

"Nathan Pitch." I extended my hand.

"Paul Glimpser," the director answered grudgingly.

Before we took it a word further, Eddie Upland swooped in out of nowhere. He seemed to already know who Glimpser was, and introduced himself before I even got a chance.

"Hi, Paul, Eddie Upland, Iceberg Productions. You're the talk of the festival. I'm a big fan of your work," he began enthusiastically. "I see you've already been coralled by our new development star here," he said, gesturing at me. Glimpser and I glowered at one another, each of us now fully blaming the other for the escalation and continuation of the situation.

"Who's your agent? I think we should do a meeting. Soon. We might have something for you to direct. Has Nathan been filling you in on our production slate?" Upland kept on, the delivery of his words giving the impression that he was touching Glimpser, intimately, all over. I started to lose my power to follow as Upland got into high wind. The V.P. pulled over every waiter that came by, gobbling the appetizers they carried, which up close were really just cubes of Wisconsin cheese, all the while slurping his drink, which was actually some cheap white wine that was being distributed in clear plastic cups. I became acutely aware of the others in the room, many now trying to maneuver for a conversation with Glimpser. I saw several people I recognized from the agency, and while I knew that Kessler was too high-profile to show up at this type of event, I sensed Shelby Stark's presence. Glimpser and I exchanged looks again, and I could swear that if we had been alone we would have tried to tear each other's throats out. Or possibly, if we were somewhere else entirely, become good friends. Upland continued to talk and eat, as if his mouth were some two-way furnace that needed to be fueled and to pour off its heat at the same time. At last Glimpser broke away after giving Upland his number and agreeing to a meeting in two days.

"Good work, Pitch," Upland said to me. "I show up and there you are, working the star of the show."

"You didn't see the screenings?" I asked.

"Nah. I had a massage appointment," he said, working his neck around. "I've been hearing a buzz on the kid for weeks, though. How was it?"

"I don't know." I shrugged.

"You were doing fine." Upland volunteered. "Maybe you just need to be a *little* more aggressive. Either that, or what I like to do is get a fix on someone's personality and replicate it back to them. NLP 'em. A little Neuro-Linguistic Programming. That way everybody thinks you're their kind of guy. Come on." My head fairly spinning, he took me by the sleeve and led me into the crowd.

For the next hour, he introduced me to dozens of film industry denizens, and from my new perch I felt a shift in my perception of the business from a Copernican to a Gallilean view. While the agency had previously been the world at the center of my universe, with agents scurrying around in its orbit to studios and producers in order to sell them their product,

I now saw how the producers scurried for product too. No single agency was of total importance. My new company's rivals were now other buyers who competed for the scarce amount of quality material. Studios could be allies, but not all the time, and writers and directors, particularly their ideas, were desperately sought. While exclusivity on the agency side—tying up a project with a single producer—was usually considered a severe limitation, from my new point of view it was suddenly highly desirable. I could not quite identify what was considered the sun at the center of this new model, and despite the introductions I hardly caught a single name. I kept throwing back the bitter white wine and waxy cheese cubes, and at each introduction I listened to Upland tell, with stuffed mouth, in increasingly glorifying terms, how his new star development guy had sewn up the meeting with the hot young director. Soon I grew queasy, but we were just getting started. Despite a quaky and hollow feeling that was seizing my guts, I attempted to stay with Upland as he continued around the room, working it, wringing it out, stringing it along, until I had to stop. I broke off and made for the bar.

I was getting some air and having a spring water over in a corner when I overheard two women. It was possible I had just met them moments before. They were fairly tall and gaunt, dressed in business attire, and young in years but had a prematurely washed-out and weary look. They were talking about Iceberg Productions. The room was loud and I was not sure, but I believe one of them was saying something about "Upland's new boy-toy." Then came their steel wool laughter. I felt humiliation gather in me as I realized Kessler's favor to me had been a loaded one. But by then they had already moved on to disparaging the present function. What happened next galvanized my attention more than even insult.

"Some affair," the taller of the women said, "not even a hint of the lovely green stuff." For an instant I assumed they were talking about a lack of serious money people at the gathering. But I had seen many rich and powerful players here. Then the other woman shined a pewter flask at her friend, and both of their faces took on languid half smiles that could only be described as beatific.

"Would you care to dance?" the one with the flask asked. She led her cohort out of the great room we were in and along a corridor. I followed at a discreet distance. They progressed down a short staircase of a half dozen steps and arrived in a small vestibule crammed with four other people. I stood at the top of the stairs and peered down at them. They were unconcerned with my presence, if they noticed it at all.

The four of them, two men and two women, all dressed in suits, had a disheveled look, and greeted the newcomers vaguely. They did not stop what they were doing, though, which was sipping cloudy emerald liquid from the clear plastic cups of the party. As they sipped, their heads tilted back in ecstasy. Their complexions shined with an unhealthy oiliness while their hair lay dull and lank on their skulls. The other women, the two new arrivals, uncorked and hurriedly shared drafts from the flask. The flask owner slumped back against the wall after drinking and seemed on the verge of tears or hysteria. Not sure what I was witnessing, I became conscious of my gawking and pulled back. I walked the corridor back toward the party, dazed by the perpetual motion of the night and all I did not know. I was looking for Upland, to say good night before making for the door, when I was set upon by Shelby Stark, who angled me into a corner near the bar.

"Nathan, Carol was so disappointed when you quit the focus groups," she said, and for a moment I was taken aback. She was all a-gray. Her skirt and sweater, and her skin as well. Her tongue was a shade of black and she gave off a murky fennel scent, and even her hair seemed to have a gray cast to it. It had been a mere five or six months since I'd last seen her, but she had the look of someone who had been living in a crypt, cold and damp. Maybe that was what the house she shared with her husband had become.

"What are you doing here?" Shelby pressed.

"I'm in development now. I just started at Iceberg," I said.

"Great for you," she said, betraying surprise, interest, and jealousy all at once. "Has Eddie Upland been chasing you around the desk yet?" she continued in a lilting tone that turned vicious.

"The hell're you're talking about?"

"You know how kneepads are standard-issue equipment for D-girls. . . . Why do you think it's any different for D-boys?" I stared at her unhealthy face and looked for something human in her gray eyes.

"Listen, Nathan, we have to schedule a lunch. Go over your production slate. And we're still due for a certain something . . . I've made men weep in bed, you know," she said huskily, her desperation suddenly taking over. Now even her forced sensuality seemed a shell of what it once was.

"Sure, Shelby, we'll get together real soon."

"Let's set a date. . . . Come on Nathan, we've known each *forever*." It had actually been nine months, and maybe that passed for forever in this town. She and I hadn't truly been friends, had only shared a somewhat unique and sordid accord, she had helped me with a job, and now she was pumping me for what *I* could provide her in a business sense. "At least," I tried to cheer myself, "I'm actually 'in play.' " But between the cheap wine, her onslaught, the unsettling allusions to Upland, and especially the strange scene I'd witnessed in the stairwell, I yearned to be away from the place.

Shelby cajoled me into promising to call her, and I withdrew myself from her withering clutches. As I waved an abbreviated good-bye to Upland from across the room, I saw Shelby moving down the corridor toward the strange drinkers I'd just seen. I went to my car and, driving home, tried to write down on paper scraps against the steering wheel some of the names and titles of people I'd met and the information I'd learned from them. I jotted a few more things while at a red light, but still felt I needed to park and unfold a large piece of paper the size of a road map to chart out all that I was seeing. After a long drought it was now flooding me in a great torrent, and I was just too tired to think anymore. So I shut off my mind and drove home by rote. I found it was easier.

The student film festival was just the beginning, though. The very next night Upland took me to an outdoor party in the backyard of a studio executive's house, held to celebrate the exec's recent promotion to president of production.

"Let's talk Tracking, Nathan," Upland said as he piloted his German sedan into Laurel Canyon toward our destination. "Let's," I said. Tracking was one of my new responsibilities as a development executive. In order to stay abreast of all the agencies and all the scripts and all the projects from all the writers and other sources, I was to engage in the vital activity of making lists of, and following, each project. "The development executive without a tracking list is as effective as an Old West sheriff without a six-gun," Upland had said to me over a protein shake and a bowl of Mueslix earlier that morning.

"You know, I have a reputation as a top tracker, a real bloodhound when it comes to hot projects in this business," Upland told me as he downshifted around a winding corner. I did not dissent.

"You've seen me do it—all day long I'll call agents and other development executives and pump them for information on upcoming scripts." He had lists broken down by agency, priority, and chronology depending on how soon a project would be available to the town. The lists indicated different levels of confidentiality surrounding each piece. The more secrecy that surrounded a script, the hotter it was considered.

"It's ironic, Eddie," I had said to Upland that morning. "A project's heat is just a reflection of how hot an agent says it is." Upland had just stared back at me with a gaze devoid of appreciation for this irony. To accept it, I suppose, would have undermined the whole process, and left him dead in the water as a tracker. He chased every piece of information like it was the golden fleece.

"You've got to learn how to plug in to the information system," Upland directed, checking the numbers of the houses along the road. "I've got one word for you, Nathan—networking," he said, glancing over at me and taking his eyes off the road for an uncomfortably long time. "You're about to witness how I secure the contacts that lead to my tracking list. Welcome to Schmoozing 101, baby. Watch and learn..." He pulled over on the side of the road behind a long string of fine sports cars and cranked up his parking brake with a ratcheting sound against the steepness of the hill. He leapt out of the car, and I followed him around the side of a large house and into the party.

On a flagstone patio surrounded by trees and centered by a tinkling fountain a throng of people drank and roared at one another. The trees were strung with tiny lights that blinked like artificial fireflies, and everyone appeared to know everyone else. From the outside this industry seemed like a large, ungainly thing, but in reality, at this party and beyond, the business was a small and incestuous world to which I had suddenly gained access. It was now expected that with practice I would build up endurance in, and develop a skill for, networking, to get to know everybody. So I went around with Upland and watched him schmooze agents, writers, other development people, producers, and studio executives, and tried to learn how to do the same myself.

Once again I watched Upland gear his manner to reflect whomever he was talking to at the moment and then ramble on without pause. He started with John Leston, an up-and-coming literary agent.

"Eddie Upland, the golden retriever," Leston began, pumping Upland's hand. "I've got to talk to you about a writing assignment. That romantic comedy you guys have . . . the remake."

"*The Lady's Fingers* . . ." Upland helped him remember our project about a gruff construction worker who ends up switching digits with a sensitive female concert pianist before they find unlikely happiness together.

"That's the one. I have a writer in mind for the job, the man I honestly believe is the single most qualified writer in town—not just amongst those whom I represent—but the entire fucking town," Leston paused for emphasis. "Jim Litwak."

Upland was poker-faced. He said nothing for a long moment.

"But then of course there is someone else equally qualified, who I happen to handle as well—Lauren Kotay," Leston said again, undaunted. "She's as much the best as he is."

Upland nodded with assurance. "They're both right at the very top of my list." He smiled and began looking over the agent's shoulder at the rest of the party. I looked too and saw we were in a very stocked pond. I saw a name partner from the biggest law firm in town, the chairman of a television network, a producing team backed by foreign money, and Charles Calloway too.

"Work the room," Upland instructed, moving off on his own, totally unaware we were not in a room. I marveled at the man's ability to slip in and out of conversation, to make acquaintances and gain ground. I wondered how long it would take me to develop similar skills.

I breathed deeply, girded myself with a potent gin and tonic from the bar, and waded into the crowd. "Hi, how are you?" I began with Will Dent, a packaging agent I recognized from my agency days. He gave me a nod and moved by. I kept at it with as many stragglers who had broken from the herd as I could, trying to gain the natural, easy intimacy all the others seemed to have. I kept on with the gin and tonics too, feeling them lubricate my handshake and smile.

I had downed more than a few before I found myself in a conversation with Liz Singleton and Maury Walsh, both studio publicists. "You watch *Random Victim*," I promised, "and you'll see a thirty-five-hundred-dollar per-screen average opening weekend." They both considered my prediction, and I added, "I come from a marketing background, so you can go to the bank on that." I could not quite believe what was coming out of my mouth. During sober moments in my past this kind of loose self-congratulatory stuff would have churned my stomach, but here I was tossing it freely.

The party went on, and I revolved around the patio fountain and back into contact with Eddie Upland. As he chased down a waitress with a tray of canapés, a small cluster of people hunched over on patio furniture at the edge of the trees caught my eye. A carafe of green liquid was passed around among them slowly. They drank deeply from it and sighed, hunching farther down toward the ground. Their aspect was similar to the stairwell dwellers I'd seen the night before. "What's with them?" I elbowed Upland.

"Absinthers." He shook his head. "Poor bastards." Absinthe. I had heard of the drink but thought it only used in

Europe a hundred years ago. Before I could inquire further, the toddler son of a major actor—Alan Asher—who had been playing precariously and unmonitored along the edge of the fountain suddenly fell in. The party froze in attention as the boy batted about in the water and swallowed great amounts of it. People broke into slow-motion gestures of movement, but no one seemed immediately able to reach the boy. Only the absinthe drinkers did not stir, did not even notice the commotion. The boy looked on his way to drowning when he was finally fished out by a nearby guest. As the guest, who I realized was a high-profile talent agent, and the crying boy walked hand in hand and dripping wet through the party toward the famous and relieved parent, Upland nudged me.

"That lucky bastard," he whispered jealously of the rescuer. "What an opportunity. He's totally in with Asher now," Upland said, referring to the star parent. I felt a prickling sense of unease creep over me at this, and at the wistful look on his face. Upland glanced around the party, searching, I thought, for a child to push into the fountain.

So began a series of days and weeks in the office and nights out on the circuit for me. So began the furthering of my education. It seemed my workdays never ended. I had to be at my desk early enough to pump New York book agents for product and stick around through dinner and drink meetings with the West Coast players. Lunch was a ritual all its own that ran, as if scripted, by a set of stock questions and witty yet just as stock responses.

"I hear you're the best," one of us would start.

"Who says that?" The other would smile. "I've gotta know where to keep sending those checks. . . . So what do you know about that new techno-thriller?"

"Well, I'll give you something on it if you put in a good word for my writing team on that preproduction polish. . . ."

At night, if I didn't have a screening to attend, then there were countless "meet the young industry" power networking get-togethers at various locations around the city. I was out swilling martinis at one of these affairs on a particular Thursday when I realized it was the night of my cousin's wedding in New York. I hadn't gone back for the occasion because I thought I couldn't afford to take the time off. But now a feeling of sadness descended on me. Months had gone by, and I was sacrificing my personal life to the business. I looked around the room at the many motivated, intelligent people—the men in crisp white shirts like me, the women in smart blue skirts—who took part in, and viewed as an integral part of their careers, something known as "schmoozing." I considered what they too were sacrificing, and for a moment I had trouble swallowing.

Late the next day, a Friday afternoon, and the secretaries had gone home. I was sitting at my desk, and Upland noticed my glum mood. "Martini flu," I offered weakly in response to his "What's wrong?"

"No, I can tell it's more than that," he pushed. "Besides, I know you can handle your martinis."

I went ahead and made the mistake of speaking my thoughts. "What we do, Eddie," I began, "it's a confidence game, isn't it?" He looked at me quizzically. "We meet somebody, make their acquaintance, and win their trust in order to simply get something—a script or information—from them. . . ." I spilled forth. If I couldn't abide by this assumed sociality that was purely commercially driven, it was my own shortcoming, I knew that, but all of a sudden I felt like a cog from the wrong factory that just didn't fit the assembly line.

Upland stiffened a little. "Just when you were doing so well . . ." he said. "I shouldn't be having second thoughts about hiring you, should I, Nathan? He moved around my desk, put a hand on my shoulder, and began kneading the tension there. "Show me I'm wrong, Nathan. Show me the lengths you're willing to go to."

I looked up at him with apprehension. I had discounted the rumors about Upland, put them down to malicious gossip, but it seemed I might have been mistaken.

"Listen," I said, and then the door to the office swung open and a mailroom delivery boy from an agency walked in. The kid looked beleaguered and miserable, no different than I had in his position. He had a script with him that was predicted to sell over the weekend, and Upland wanted to get a copy of it to the principal of the company, that elusive Jumper Sussman. We hoped he would read it and possibly bid on it.

"I'll take it over to Jumper on my way home," I offered. I wanted to get away from Upland and to meet the man in charge, who had not yet stopped by the office. "I was ready to leave anyway." Upland could say nothing.

Arriving at the wrought iron entryway to Sussman's secluded and very large home and grounds, I picked up the phone that waited near the mailbox, announced who I was, and watched as the gates swung open. I drove up a brick, lighted driveway that housed several unremarkable American cars parked next to several other very remarkable British and Italian automobiles. Preparing myself with clever lines to use upon meeting Sussman, I shouldn't have been surprised when an aged Asian houseman, his arms full of fine woman's garments, came outside to take the package. I talked briefly with the diminutive old man, who said his name was Kai, and waited while he loaded the clothes into one of the American cars. It was a Jeep, and it reminded me of an article I had read in a recent "Calendar" section of the *Times* discussing the new down-to-earth trend of celebrities and other power brokers to drive solid, practical four-wheel-drive vehicles rather than luxury cars. Sussman's wife, in fact, had been profiled in the article. I mentioned the article to Kai, who told me she had never driven, or even ridden in, their Jeep before.

"She no want to use a car without a phone in it. And she no put one because she do not want us help to make calls," he said.

"What's with the clothes?" I asked, noticing that the tags were still attached. One of Kai's longtime duties, he related to me in his broken English, was to take expensive clothing that Sussman's wife had bought, and worn with the tags tucked discreetly away, back to stores and return them for refund. As for his own clothing habits, Sussman was said to wear the same shabby slacks and shirt daily, along with drab shoes that had developed holes in their bottoms from overuse. Rather than this displaying an admirable frugality in his fabulously wealthy employers, Kai tried to stress there was a malicious tightness at work here.

"Cheep, cheep," he repeated over and over, complaining about his long hours and forced weekend work without overtime pay. As he spoke I realized that not only was I not going to meet Sussman, I wasn't even going to be invited inside the house. Soon after, I drove off, wishing the valet a good weekend.

The episode itself would have been meaningless if it hadn't set the precedent of my now having to make deliveries to Sussman's house. Upland, perhaps suspicious of my commitment, perhaps annoyed at my dodging his advance, had me continue to bring scripts to Sussman's house. "It'll save the company some money on messengers, and it's not that far out of your way, right, Nathan?" Upland said in a tone I recognized too well from my mailroom days. I had managed to put myself back on a mail route. The trips did nothing for my career, nor did they add to my knowledge of the business. They only allowed me to increasingly become a confidant to the browbeaten Kai, who willingly offered stories about working for Sussman. Stories which drew a strange portrait of the absent producer.

At first I didn't overly concern myself with the talk, considering it just staff grumbling, until one afternoon I arrived with some videotape reels of directors Sussman was thinking of hiring. As I sat in my car in the driveway, I witnessed the tearful departure of the latest in a long string of briefly tenured Mexican chambermaids. Inside the gated mansion, Kai told me, it was one of the maids' jobs to ensure that only full rolls of toilet paper resided in the master, guest, and ancillary bathrooms. All rolls less than half full, right on down to the cardboard, had to be placed in the servants' quarters for their use. The effort these people, the Sussmans, would go to in order to evade even the pathetic reality of a spent roll of ass-wipe staggered me. And the tyranny toward those poor Mexican maids. Living in a castle, but forever, repeatedly pulling the last few sheets right down to the spindle, and cruelly never being able to enjoy the luxury of a proper handful of tissue. In addition, the first sheet of each new roll was to be folded into a point, grand hotel style, at Mrs. Sussman's command. This last assignment had been forgotten by the maid one too many times, and so she had been served with her walking papers.

The tales from Kai, along with those I heard from Sussman's secretary, seemed to confirm what I'd realized—that I had yet to meet a rich and powerful man who enjoyed a happy life. These stories of my absentee boss seemed to foretell of a sick future for anybody foolish enough to pursue a fortune in this town. As time passed I also began to feel development was in itself a ridiculous concept. Over and over I redoubled my efforts to do my job and find great scripts, but none of our projects were moving forward. It seemed that I bent down and put my nose in a script, and when I looked up it was three months later, and then six, and little had changed. I had networked myself with agents, writers, and other development people, but I realized that although I'd been around the business for a while now, I still did not *know* anyone who had actually made a real film. Exciting ones were popping out all the time, but they always seemed to have been done by someone else whom I had merely heard of or read about in the trades.

I began to believe the only thing that could be truly satisfying about the business was actual production—the promised land, the holy grail. I had almost forgotten all about it in my efforts to become a smooth networker, but making movies was the reason I was here. The idea that one of the projects I had been working on, writing notes on, and receiving draft after draft of, would finally be green-lighted and would begin to be made into a film, was the hope upon which I hinged my peace of mind. Nothing ever seemed to happen, though, and I finally came to understand my version of the sailor's doldrums. Coming to work every day and going through the motions, I was thwarted. I felt I was on an antique schooner in the tropics, sails flaccid for weeks in the slowly rocking waves, water and provisions and sanity dwindling. As I waited for a healthy, life-giving breeze to billow the canvas and send me along on my way again, I began to feel paralyzed. The state I was in was floridly called "development hell," though it seemed "development purgatory" was more apt. It described the interminable enthusiasm-eroding, life-eroding wait for a studio to launch and finance a picture. Not only did a script have to be either good, or just commercially viable, a reputable director securely on board, decent actors that would ensure some box office receipts attached, but the studio head's bowels had to be regular and the planets in alignment for a green light to be given. The rest was just waiting.

• • •

Before long an evil and tenacious feeling of boredom set in. I made forays into the market for other jobs, but with my experience still limited, I found no real opportunities. I was stuck in a cycle of industry functions that had grown painfully redundant, networking that now felt pointless, and the useless tuning of scripts that would never make the transition to the screen. I looked around and saw hundreds in my stratum of the business stuck just like me. Late one morning, on my way to a lunch, Upland, supposedly hard at work on his computer, called out from his office. "How do you spell 'doodling'?"

"Two o's and two d's," I said, feeling my job, and maybe my life, had become absurd.

"Okay," he went on, "and what's another six-letter word for 'vacant'?" As I walked out of the office to my appointment, I felt a landslide, a cave-in deep inside me. I was at a loss to understand what had caused it so palpably and so all at once, but I could not escape it.

I sat down to my chopped salad and lunch patter with Tim Moshefsky, a fellow director of development from another company. Moshefsky had spaces between his teeth and freckles. His once white shirt had been overlaundered and was faintly blue. His fountain pen ran out of ink as he titled a notecard "Lunch w/Pitch," and he had to borrow a ballpoint from our waitress. Glancing under the table, I saw only one of his preppy loafers held a penny, and there was something unaccountably sad about this picture.

"What's the word on 'Bully Boys'?" Tim wondered about a rumored Mafia project. I looked at him and considered the system. Common sense dictated that when bartering project titles and information, one received the same in return as one gave. But at that pace, one tiny piece at a time, none of us was going to get anywhere. I couldn't expect this guy, this earnest jug-eared worker, to do any more than the usual for me. Then I found myself with a new idea, one that would have made me an object of derision from Andrew Carnegie to T. Boone Pickens right on to my father. I took out the tracking list, twelve pages thick, that Upland and I spent our precious time and used valuable contacts compiling, and handed it to Moshefsky.

He choked on a nub of oil-dipped bread when he realized what I was doing. He began to try to transcribe it onto his little notecard, but I stopped him.

"Keep it," I said.

"I can't . . . you know . . . repay this in kind," he stammered at his good fortune. I waved off his gratitude. Perhaps he'd be the one to secure some great script from the list and will it forward into production as Upland and I had been unable to do. Upland would have sacked me immediately had he known about it. He would have seen my actions as treasonous or just plain stupid, and I didn't know which would get me fired faster. It wasn't either of those things, though. I just couldn't bear playing this guy, or any others who were scrabbling so hard to climb up the same ladder I was, any longer. I didn't want to hold out on them anymore, even though they were holding out on me. I suddenly wanted to connect with any one of them on an honest level or not at all. But they wouldn't have time for me if I didn't have something good to offer, so rather than bait the whole thing along one scrap at a time, I decided to give it all right up front, and then I would see if anything came of it.

I repeated my actions at several lunches over the next weeks. The stunned gratitude of my fellow diners was only outstripped by their paranoid suspicions that a trick was being played. And the bitter part of it, the part that furthered my sickening with the development process altogether, was that nothing ever did come of it. I did not see any films progress toward being made from those coveted lists. I did not cultivate anything other than the most superficial relationships with these people, who had no concern with going beyond that. It was like pouring water into dry sand. The more I poured, the more they seemed to absorb, until long after the vessel was empty. Long after. But wasn't that always the way it was with love? It was what, I had to admit to myself, my actions revealed. In this most unlikely of places a vague, senseless, unrequited love for my fellow citizens of the business had sprung up. At first I told myself I had performed my information donations nonchalantly, possibly with a touch of generosity and a stylish unwillingness to pander to the system, somewhat out of scorn, with a dashing touch of disgust, and even a little rebellious hate thrown in, but these were just different degrees of the same thing. Compassion. Underlying this myriad of reasons was simply a great need to be amongst my fellows, to help them. I did not recognize from where this new passion came. I never suspected myself of possessing anything like it. To last at all in this town, I knew it must be extinguished, and had I stood accused, I would have surely denied its existence. For the first time since I'd arrived here, I believed my mother might be proud of me.

CHAPTER FIVE

Late a hot July Friday night found me ready to leave the office for another industry flesh-pressing session at Asylum, a trendy restaurant-bar that would only be *en vogue* for a moment in this town with its cruelly short attention span. I stood and gazed out at the insistent lights of the city for a long time, then flicked off my desk lamp. I gathered a tall pile of twelve scripts, my weekend read, and headed for the door. As I passed through the office foyer I caught a glimpse of myself in the mirror there. I was not enchanted with what I saw. The long, unproductive hours had registered on me. I was puffy around the face, my skin was pale, a purpling had set in beneath my eyes. My hair had a little too much grease product in it, and my hand-painted floral-patterned tie was loud. The salesman had said the tie's bright colors "greeted people," which was why I bought it, but looking at it now I decided it rather yelled "Hi!" right into one's face. I could only shrug, stuff my wrinkled shirttail back into my pants, readjust the hefty bundle of scripts against my hip, and leave.

I pushed open the tremendous hammered copper doors of Asylum and proceeded through the chiaroscuro lighting of the dining room. I walked past tables of diners whose heads swiveled to spot each new arrival. Moving through a velvet curtained entrance into the dark and woody-hued bar area, I could hear the din of a crowd, as well as a jazz combo tuning up. Though I had arrived late, even later than the fashionable—which was everybody—I planned on leaving early. The occasion of a development-person mixer was a blatant way for D-people to increase their contact base, traffic in dirty favors, and oftentimes get laid, and I had attended far too many of them over the past months. Looking around, I saw some agents were in attendance as well, and their presence would only add to the painfully workmanlike feel of the evening.

I slid onto a corner bar stool, waving hello to several people I knew. Many of them had benefited from my tracking list like Tim Moshefsky had, but rather than gratitude I felt enmity flowing from them, for though I'd given each of them information, word had gotten around I hadn't given it to each exclusively. The combo fired up a tired "Stormy Monday"–type jazz standard as I considered the twinkling selection of bottles aligned on the wall in front of me. Shelby Stark interrupted as I signaled to the bartender, sashaying over to me, her movements loose with intoxication. If she had looked gray the last time I had seen her, she was even more winnowed this time. The sun, or the lack of sun, her life, or her lack of the same had blanched her to a dun color close to that of dust. She settled onto the bar stool next to mine and seemed as precarious as a pillar of that very substance. An unexpected breeze and she might have blown away completely.

"So, are congratulations or condolences in order?" she began, showing me the wintry pickets of her smile.

"Shelby, you've got to take some time off," I said.

"You and me both," she answered, nudging into me sloppily with an elbow.

I leaned as far away as my bar stool would allow, eyes trained on the bartender. "Gin and tonic," I pleaded.

"Is it me, or have you gone gay?" she blurted out.

"I'm all career, Shelby, I don't have time for anything else," I said, hoping that would do.

"Will you have more time soon?" she inquired.

"What do you mean?" I asked, confused, remembering how she had opened the conversation.

"Don't you know?" she asked.

"Obviously not."

"Your company just took a deal at a certain major studio. It's on the grapevine," she said with the smugness that accompanied being in-the-know.

"Which studio?" I wondered aloud in my surprise.

"Would Jumper Sussman settle for anything other than the best?" she said. Only one studio, one backed by Japanese money and on a glorious spring and summer run of hits, could be considered tops right now. It would mean a daily trip to the Valley for me. A trip I only hoped I would be making.

"The question is, are you going along?" she pondered.

"That is the question," I agreed, drifting into thought about my fate. As bleak as the job had become, the idea of being umemployed again hung like a black chasm at the edge of my thoughts. I well remembered the financial strain and lack of ballast during my last workless stint. The recollection caused me to double the strength of my drink order, which I signaled to the bartender with a wrist-twisting motion. Several of my counterparts from other companies began to crowd the bar around me before Shelby could have more sport with me, and she eventually drifted away. During the course of their ordering drinks, the D-people tore at me hyena-like with questions about my company's move.

"Have you heard the news?" Terry Fahrenbach, a red-headed director of development for an independent producer, inquired.

"Of course," I answered, trying to protect my flanks, "you think I'm out of the loop?"

"You had to have seen this coming, Nathan. It's been two years, and Upland hasn't gotten anything into production. . . ."

"Oh, I saw it coming. Don't you worry about that."

By the time I finished my second drink, I was slapping my questioners on the back with reassurance and talking about the company's new offices, and after a few more I was responding, "Jumper and I discussed the move in detail." I would add a narrowing of the eyes and a knowing nod, although my hopes of keeping my job were sinking with each passing round. Finally I began to stiffen on my bar stool. The place began emptying out, and I moved to a small table near a cavernous but dormant fireplace where I could brood over my situation in peace.

Sitting there swirling ice cubes in my glass, I was curious to see a few D-people I vaguely recognized nearby order hot tea and glasses of ice water. Their collars fit loosely around their necks, and they were quite pale in comparison to the last time I had seen them. Many D-people spent their weekends searing on the beach, hunkered down in the sand with a stack of scripts, but not this pasty group. When their order arrived, they discarded the small teapots and instead poured cold water into the teacups. One of them produced a silver hip flask and poured from it into the teacups clandestinely beneath the table. They stirred in sugar and drank. They reminded me of kids spiking drinks at a junior high school dance, though there was something both more jovial and sinister in their manner. I knew they were using absinthe. I had been considering leaving, but was now fascinated and ready to watch them. I'd been hearing more about the drink, but had yet been presented with an opportunity to try it.

After they had imbibed for a moment all conversation at the table ceased, and their jaws lowered and lowered and finally just hung. There was a detached indolence to them, as they seemed joined in the same far-off place. My curiosity had grown with each exposure I'd had to absinthe drinkers, but it was this impression of distance that made me hesitate in approaching them. Just then a waiter, uniformed like a cossack, stopped at my table.

"Compliments of a young lady," he said, referring to a drink, a glass of champagne, he placed in front of me.

"Interesting," I uttered. "Who?"

"She asked me not to say, sir," he informed me, hurrying away.

I was still waiting for an approach a half hour later, and the immediate thrill had worn off. The group of mysterious drinkers was gone, having muttered bitterly over running out of absinthe before leaving. The dregs of the grueling forced-meeting boredom washed weakly around me. I had drained the champagne, the last of a series of drinks much greater than I hazily remembered promising myself I would take in a single night. Especially gin. It wasn't that promises like these were so hard to keep, they were just so hard to remember. Once again I was about to leave when the waiter came back and put down a fresh glass and a bottle of champagne resting in a silver ice bucket.

"Look," I said, "I'll give you fifty to tell me who she is."

"She gave me a hundred not to tell you, sir," the waiter answered. "She said she'll come talk to you at the end of the night."

"Send her whatever she's drinking," I said, handing the waiter the fifty that could have been all his, a fifty that I should have earmarked for food, or my electric bill, or some other necessary thing. The bribe was a feeble attempt to gain control of the encounter, but I had made it without regret. "Don't worry, pal," I said to the indecision in the waiter's eyes, "I won't watch you deliver it. I'm a better sport than that."

The situation caused me to flash on Feller. Although he had made agent, I had not heard a thing about him lately. He was never present at these types of events, and I wondered if he was out of the circle, or in a more high-powered one. Either way, Feller would definitely be the type to watch where the waiter delivered the drink, betraying the mystery, taking all the sacrament out of the ritual.

"By the way, I'm not making it to closing time . . . and keep the change," I said, my interest in the situation overriding my judgment.

"If I may say, sir, you'd give me a hundred too if you saw her." The waiter smiled as he hustled away, and a few minutes later, as if she sensed exactly when I had had it and was going to leave, she crossed the room.

She was not a beauty if one was a purist, which I certainly wasn't. She had a little too much nose, and her eyes, shimmering hazel, were the slightest bit too close together. That was about it for flaws, except for a less than perfect smile due to her eyeteeth being quite pointed. Her eyes were deep, though, and very plaintive when she turned them on me. So plaintive, in fact, that when she used them, and it was obvious when she did, they worked on me anyway.

She strode my way with a confidence that must have been trumped up, and gave me the eyes and a line. "Well, I paid the toll so . . ." she began, seeming not at all nervous.

"A hundred bucks," I remarked aloud as I took the cool, smooth hand she offered.

"What?"

"Nothing. Nathan Pitch."

"Ronnie Sylvan," she said, as if she knew exactly what it all meant.

"So, would you like to join me for a drink?" I asked.

"I thought I did, but seeing you up close . . . I don't know, you kind of look like a man in between," she teased. She appraised me cautiously for a moment, and I did the same back to her with less caution. She was slim, about a size on the upside of petite, with addictive curves a little more present than the word subtle might describe. She was wearing what was popularly known as a cat suit, a close-fitting black sheath of fabric that encouraged the illicit imagination. At last she sat down.

"Maybe I am. Just in the career sense, though," I mused.

"Well, what is it you do?" she asked.

"I'm in development. Iceberg Productions." I swallowed.

"Oh. I'm sorry. Do you have anything else lined up?" she said, not seeming sorry at all.

"What do you mean, 'sorry'?"

"*I* heard that the vice president isn't surviving the move, so . . ." she said, haughty as an alley cat.

"Well, I guess it's a good thing I'm not the vice president." I matched her tone, causing her eyes to sparkle. "I work for him."

"I see."

"So now that you know who I'm not, do you know anything about who I am? Do I have a job, for instance?" I asked. I wondered if Upland was aware that he was already a casualty.

"Let me make a call," she said, taking out an impossibly small cellular phone that did not get reception in the bar. She held up one delicate finger, showing me how long I'd need to wait until her return, and stood. As she walked away, spinning through the tightly arranged tables, I was allowed a full minute's appreciation of her. Anyone who'd been around for more than a week could see right away that she was loaded with everything necessary to go all the way in this business, that she was trouble in a town full of trouble girls.

The waiter came back to the table, vigilantly attending to my drink needs. I now loved this waiter above all other waiters, for whom I felt strongly already. Not the ones with a grand plan, the actor waiters, but legitimate working waiters. They were better off than the delusional grand planners anyway. They could always wait tables; they didn't need a lucky break or an audience. They were more like writers, who could always write regardless of who was reading it, or readers, for that matter, who could always just read. I pitied the actors, for they never got a chance to act; they just waited for an opportunity to do anything at all. The only people worse off, more at someone else's mercy than actors, were directors. They didn't just need a job; they needed to be made boss, and they needed great amounts of money to practice their trade. And D-people, I was beginning to suspect, D-people might be the poorest off of all, for even when we were doing our job, we weren't really doing anything other than carrying out an abstract theory—development. Now, however, it was very possible I would no longer be paid for being an abstraction, and the only thing worse than being an abstraction was being one of the unpaid variety.

Regardless of the outcome of my job situation, I thought, quaffing the frigid and tangy champagne, I knew now that I was going to have to work on my flexibility as an industry soldier. I would need to make myself more useful on more fronts. I would have to become so damn flexible that they'd call me Plastic Man. I would also have to bolster my immunity to the bullshit, I thought, already redoubling my efforts to mentally vaccinate myself against it. The key was in making my whole self a differentially permeable membrane, to let in the good stories, smart people, worthwhile experiences, and to shut out the slag material, hustlers, and tawdry scenes. To not let them get to me. Flexibility. Immunity. Permeability. I repeated it to myself, then Ronnie came back to the table.

"Well?"

"I don't know exactly what's in store for you, but you're not in the same boat as the V.P. . . . ."

"Upland."

"Right, Upland," she said, lifting her glass. "Cheers to survival, then." We touched glasses and sipped. "You like?"

"The champagne?"

"It's not champagne, it's Cristal."

I brushed by her affectation. "So what is it you do that gets you all this good information?"

"I'm a personal manager."

"Why not agenting?" I wondered.

"Agents take ten percent and can't be aboard as producer." She smiled, lighting up again.

"Managers take more and can," I finished for her, beginning to understand her better by the second.

"Blossom Management." She smiled over her glass at me. "I have a few select clients. I own the shop." I recognized the name of the concern, and it did indeed handle a few very impressive clients. "I get one movie made, I cover my nut for ten years," she finished. Agents couldn't do that. "So should we move on?"

"You seem to know more about my fate than I do," I half joked.

"Let's go, then," she said, once again offering me her small, well-manicured hand. It had been a long while since I had let my cock do my thinking for me, and as I took her hand, I forgot just how stupid it could be.

Once outside we decided to go to Chartreuse, an after-hours café she liked, for late supper. I struggled to follow the taillights of her Mercedes convertible as she sped along Sunset past the plaza and we passed through the ugliness of the city, which tonight seemed not so ugly as lively. I arrived moments behind and settled close beside her in a tiny booth in time to watch as she ordered an assortment of rich dishes for us despite the late hour. She chose *pâté de fois gras*, *canapés*, and *steak tartare*, followed by a *friseé* and *lardon* salad, *bouillabaisse*, and *Grand Marnier soufflé* for dessert. The food began to arrive quickly, but not before she rushed on into conversation. She spoke in vague, clipped pronouncements about her values, which orbited around, and fed, her top priority—herself—and even my time in the business hadn't prepared me for it.

"In this business it's position to perception and perception of position," she started off, loading a toast point with pâté. "For me as much as for my clients," she continued, feeding me the rich liver. As I chewed and listened, she talked on about her position in town, which was a strong one, and the types of careers she had engineered for her clients, influential and emerging actors. I gathered through her hints, intentional and unintentional, that she was extremely successful.

"There's a lifestyle I've become accustomed to—and it's called freedom." She smiled seductively, her words seeming validated by her accomplishments in deal making. "And money buys me that freedom."

"Don't you mean 'lends'?" I asked, sampling the *tartare*, the idea of which had repulsed me prior to this night.

"Buys," she stated emphatically. "That's why I don't like accountants. I'd never date one. They don't understand."

"No accountant? No matter what?" I wondered.

"No. You've got to draw lines, Nathan," she said, tasting each dish with enthusiastic appreciation, leaving them all tested but unfinished.

"Don't you want to eat more?" I wondered as she pushed the full plates away.

"That's my secret, to always stay hungry." I nodded in assent, which she did not believe.

"Look, this is my theory. I consider my life is a vehicle, like a car, and the money affords me all the options. Like power steering, cruise control . . . For instance, my Mercedes," she said, of the vehicle she had driven here, "is my fifth car."

"Your fifth life?"

"No, this time I mean car," she sighed, frustrated with me. "It's all about building on what you've got. Accruing. What I really want is a diamond Cartier cat, a second home, *property* . . ." Her talk would have been altogether heartless, bloodless, if it had been affected in the least, but even her affectation seemed a part of her nature.

As the plates were cleared, she told me how she spent time with certain wealthy, much older men, and thought they could show her what fun and excitement were, what life was. She knew she was a Republican "regardless of candidate." This, I interpreted, was something else she'd learned from them.

"You talk about money like it's going out of style." I shook my head as the dessert arrived.

"As if it ever could . . ." She smirked, skipping the soufflé but spooning the *zabignone* right into her luscious mouth.

"Well, then," I said, trying to join in, to somehow match her, "my vehicle, the one I'm looking for, isn't a car, or even a jet airplane, but a starship. A hurtling spacecraft." I groped in alcohol-bred inexactness for a hint of transcendence. I was not optimistic about my chances with her.

"I like that," she said, surprising me. "That's something a much older man would say."

"Sometimes, though, I want to chuck it all and travel, just leave and see the world. . . ." She sighed wistfully, seemingly taking my lead. She displayed her side of sweet kindness as a butcher would a London broil—for a moment, and then it was back behind the glass. "But I don't know where I want to go, so I stay and do what I do." By then she had leaned close, allowing me to smell her fragrant smell and become blinded by her gleaming skin. "The truth is, I can't just leave, because I live for the kill." She said it with steel in her voice, before refreshing her bright lipstick. I saw then she was most like a hawk, and for all my insouciant attitude, I was a small rodent in a field being rapidly covered by the dark shadow of her wings, too struck by the spectacle of her to bother fleeing. On an impulse I put my hand behind her head, grasped her lustrous hair, and pulled her face toward mine. I kissed her with muted aggression, smearing her newly applied lipstick. She surprised me by opening her mouth midway through the kiss, and her teeth contacted mine with force. When I pulled away, she smiled mildly and blotted her mouth, ruining the purity of her linen napkin.

"Where the hell're you from?" I asked, wondering where someone like her was created.

"From here," she said, spreading her arms expansively. I believe she was the first native of the town I had ever met.

It was time to leave, and she picked up the check, squelching my protest with swift logic about my unknown work status. I felt I'd taken on the role of kept man when out at the cars she suggested we should retire to someone's place. "How about yours?" I said, not eager to open the cracker box to any outside scrutiny.

"Fine," she said, "but mine's being painted, so I'm staying at a hotel." She was so cool about it, I just got into my car and followed her, and it was much later before I considered whether or not this was true.

Arriving in front of the L'Ermitage moments later, I, for a split second, felt victim to some elaborate conspiracy. I flipped my keys to the valet with a dash of fateful spirit and walked into the lobby a step behind her. They did seem to know her at the desk, and the clerk handed her a key wordlessly and with immediacy, although she slid something back across the

counter toward him. Up in the room, I felt the chill of conspiracy again. Most rooms in a hotel had a similar layout, it
was true, but this particular hotel was known to take pains to
individualize each room with different art and slightly varying
furniture. Yet I was sure this was the same room I had been
in with Mrs. Kessler. Ronnie opened another bottle of champagne from the bar refrigerator and seemed at home in the
room, though none of her belongings were visible. I really was
not up to thinking much more about ramifications, fairly going
under from the lateness and drink, and forgot everything when
she took me behind the swirling gossamer curtain that separated the bedroom from the living room.

In the elegant bedroom her tongue beat like a gypsy but-
terfly at my ear. I turned out the dimmed lights, and she pulled
me down onto the canopied bed. It was like falling through
the old into a new land. Her mouth was hot and soft, and
every part of her was luminous and liquid.

"I have lines in here too that you're not to cross," she
breathed as I raced to unclothe her. "The panties don't come
off, dear," was the first one. But she didn't resist daring me
anyway, because "You know how much I want you" was one
of the first things she said, just after telling me, "You're not
getting it all, you know."

"Who said I want it all?" I gamely replied, because I'm
a gamer. I peeled her out of the cat suit and was wounded
by the perfection there. The planes of her body dipped and
rolled beneath my hands. Her skin was the skin that was
intended when the Creator of the world conceived of skin. I
applied myself to the abandoned touching of her in the hope

she would abandon herself and her rules. And she talked about reciprocating. Talked about it.

"What turns you on?" she wondered. "What makes you crazy?" she demanded, trying to take the easy way. But I was good, I was, and I knew that if I told her, if I let her take the easy way, it would bore her, and I'd be slaughtered.

"You'll figure it out," I croaked. I knew she would, and then I could just forget about it. It was not foreplay between us. More like the first few moments of a heavyweight fight. The old-style kind, fifteen rounds. Everybody in the room knows that serious leather's going to be thrown, but not yet, and they're going to have to wait.

"Powerhouse fucking is what it will be between us," I said, knowing it would be, and knowing I could say it since she moaned when *she* kissed me and bit my chest.

I learned what it felt like to be in someone's sights when she turned to me and said, "You like to play hardball, don't you?" and then, not waiting for a reply, "You give so much and take so little in here, you try to break a woman, what's your game?"

"It's about control . . . I like to keep it . . . because I'm married," I lied. I couldn't tell her that I'd been both looking for her and terrified of finding her since I'd arrived here. No, then she would have had me in the gutter picking after cigarette butts and loose change.

She snorted with absolute disbelief. "Well, a lot of men have called me the perfect mistress. Three have written screenplays about me. The best of them—he's been nominated for an Oscar—gave up his attempt altogether."

"You're no screenplay," I uttered. "You're a Borges story." She liked this and signaled that rules would be broken, that there would be exceptions now. The panties, wisp-like things, were discarded, rolled excruciatingly down her taut thighs, which she parted as she gave herself to me. I plunged forward, like a stone dropping down a deep well, into an abyss so disgustingly pleasurable that it brought a feeling near nausea up from my stomach to the back of my throat.

Later, a long time after we were finished, she hummed and stroked me, and the contradictions were too much. Passion and depth melded with crass ambition; one part of her had to be an act. I felt she must be grifting me.

"I still don't have your number. How am I supposed to call you?" she asked as I lay on the edge of the bed. I wondered if this was her trying to assure me.

"It's not like we would have such a great phone rapport," I said, instinctively knowing that it was time to put back up the buffers, that the only way to keep her interested was to keep her off balance.

"Yeah, but we have a great bed rapport," she volleyed back.

"Listen," I said, turning to her with seriousness, "all the stupid trash you talk, like some female executive Godzilla caricature, you mean it." I grew nearly miserable with the realization.

"Maybe it's all just a trick." She smiled. It was all so contrived, every last choreographed bit of it, but like a magic show or great film—illusion had become reality, and then even more real.

"Then what's the point?" I wondered.

"You need someone to work out your demons on," she said, though I was sure she would create more than I'd be able to purge.

"What's in it for you?" I asked. "What do you want in return?"

"Just that you think about me when we're together," she said finally, and then we didn't talk anymore.

I lay there in silence for a long while, feeling her next to me, and realized with a chill that what I'd seen her slide across the hotel's front desk was a credit card. Then, as if reading my thoughts, she laughed. Laughed aloud in the darkness. It was a fantastic sound, dreamy and savage, innocent yet depraved. I recognized it. It came from the same mean, burned-out place where my own now issued. It made me long to hear a young, weightless laugh again. One to which I could attribute the word *tinkling*. I no longer believed that kind of laugh existed. I knew less how to find it. Although I had grown afraid, I did not move until I knew she was asleep, and then I stood and began looking for my clothes.

CHAPTER SIX

On Monday morning, after getting my pass at the gate and driving onto the studio grounds, I felt I had entered a theme-park version of a college campus. Boys in preppy shirts and girls in plaid skirts pushed mail carts and rode bicycles with baskets to and fro. New and old buildings alike had ivy clinging to their sides. There was a labored but palpable feeling of nostalgia about the place, with small exhibits displaying characters, images, and stars that forced association with the studio's golden past. There was a store that sold discounted memorabilia of historic films, and whether it was all there for visitor tours or to boost employee morale, I could not tell. Walking down the backlot streets that went from Old-Time-Big-City, to Main-Street-America, to Old-West around single corners, I had to step aside for several golf carts that rolled by carrying cast and crew from dressing trailers to sets housed in the airplane hangar–sized sound stages. There were red "taping" lights controlling entry outside sound stage doors, and when one blinked on while I watched, it ignited my excitement at the possibility I would actually be working at the studio. The entire place was suffused with a sense of "yes, it's work, but we like it too."

Two nights back, upon my return home from the hotel, I had been furry-headed from lack of sleep, and my mouth had a coating from the drinking and the rest. As I moved through my apartment in the half-light of dawn, the shade of light witnessed after only the most wonderful of nights or the most horrible, my answering machine blinked a jeering red, and I moved to check it. I had several messages from Upland, like communiqués from the front of an increasingly bloody battle. The first was just "Pitch, it's Eddie Upland, please call me."

The next, "It's Eddie again, some things have been going on." After that they grew frantic, as if he were calling for air support while mortar rounds were walked in on his position somewhere in the South Pacific. "Nathan, something's up with the company. It's a real bitch. You have my number." The last one was a resigned "The shit's hit the fan. Calling to see how you made out," and I could practically smell the smoke curling up from his lost, bombed-out hut. I forwarded through them, finally arriving at the last message on the tape, this from Jumper Sussman's prim and handsome secretary, Jackie. It instructed me to report to a location at the studio early Monday morning; a drive-on pass would be left for me at the gate. That was it. Beep. I figured they wouldn't have me report on Monday just to give me a pink slip, that maybe I was getting a chance.

As I was early for my appointment, I headed to the commissary for a cup of coffee. Waiting in line, I watched work-boot–wearing tech crewmen load their trays with three-course, heavy-starch breakfasts, cigarettes burning all the while. Seeing the thick, lumpy gravy they ladled onto weighty-looking biscuits did nothing for my appetite, which was minimal to begin with. My nerves were pecking away at my stomach, a result of the early morning briskness of the studio, the physical proximity to my dust-covered dream of actual filmmaking, and the residual neuron charges firing throughout my system in the aftermath of my evening with Ronnie Sylvan.

We hadn't spoken since I had left her at the hotel and stepped out into that bruised dawn. But I hadn't stopped thinking about her either. I was sure there was a deep well of shimmering emotion within her waiting to be tapped. I believed that the deep erotic connection we had made must be impossible without this. I had taken her number, even used it, dialing six digits and hanging up a few times in a feeble attempt at self-preservation. I had finally let the call go through and reached her answering machine, hanging up on it without leaving a message, not willing to relinquish the tiny bit of control I fancied I could maintain by not being the one to call. After getting her machine a few more times through Sunday, I believed she really was having her place painted and tried her at the hotel. She wasn't there either, though, and they gave me no information as to when she had checked out.

I swallowed the commissary coffee, letting it flow down over the chunks of coal that were my stomach, then walked out beneath the cheerful maples that lined the walk to the Producers Building. Moving down the hall, I was impressed by the uniformity of each wing, and took several wrong turns through glass doors sheltering well-known production companies, which resulted in my asking for directions two times. I had memories of the mailroom, racing along my delivery route even more lost than I was now, Jared breathing down my beeper all the while. Before long, though, I found the suites, spacious skeleton caverns of future luxury, that would soon house Iceberg Productions.

A few phone-installation men walked in wearing studio golf shirts with tool belts around their waists, and worked on the jacks, taking no notice of me, just another suit to them. I *was* something of a suit too, edgy, eager, and willing to dig in at this place and work. I had attempted to clear my mind over the past two days by not reading a single script, the longest time I had abstained in recent memory. I was endeavoring to renew my vigor for the process, telling myself that as tiresome as it had become, it was what I did well, maybe what I did best. I wanted to be ready for the familiar challenge of cracking a second act structural problem in my script notes, or nailing a main character's dramatic arc.

Just as I began to wonder if I had gone to the wrong office, I heard approaching footsteps and the sound of Jackie's voice. She was dressed for action in a gray suit and clutched a clipboard. Arriving with her was a male decorator dressed in pastels and carrying thick books of fabric samples and furniture designs. I was glad to see Jackie's familiar face.

"Hello, Nathan, Mr. Sussman will be up momentarily," she

said, and then they left me and continued on into another part of the suite, talking about layout.

So I was finally going to meet him, the elusive Jumper Sussman. Legend had it that years ago Jumper had gotten his sobriquet due to his rapid advancement out of a talent agency mailroom to agent past a horde of other trainees. His subsequent rise through a studio's ranks all the way to chief, then a stint as an independent producer, had validated it. At least that was what he'd have people believe. I happened to have learned, listening to a Kessler phone call, that Jumper had actually come up with the name. In a bizarre assertion of fancy and will over true identity he had renamed himself after college.

A moment later I heard half of a conversation being yelled loudly, and in a New York accent. A smallish gray-haired man with a bit of a belly and a bit more of a tan, wearing conservative but disheveled clothes, entered the space where I was waiting. He was shouting into a cellular phone with little effect.

"Hold on," he said to the party on the other end, and turned to the phone man, now in mid-installation. "Hey, pal, what are the chances you get that thing on-line during this call?" he said.

The worker just shook his head and continued his task. "Sorry," he said, not meaning it.

The producer looked at me, and we both shrugged our shoulders. Back to his conversation, Sussman yelled, "Nothing works where I'm at. Story of my life. Hello? Hello, Saul?" Turning back to me, clicking off the cellular and pushing in its short antenna, Sussman muttered, "Damn thing," and then, "So, kid, you must be young Pitch."

"Mr. Sussman," I said, extending my hand.

"I could tell by the tie," Sussman said in a flat way that left me unsure about whether I was expected to laugh, thank him, or apologize.

"I didn't know you were from New York."

"Brooklyn. All the great ones are from New York," the man stated. "You?"

"Queens," I said, and appraised the producer. He was completely unassuming, which immediately convinced me of the power he wielded. In a business full of hype artists, frauds, and gasbags, this man actually seemed understated.

"What do you think of the new digs?" Sussman asked.

"Nice. Roomy," I said, eliciting a snort of laughter from him.

"Yeah, well, we're fixing them up. My wife's coming in to meet with the decorator. Then we can get some work done."

"Is the deal first-look or exclusive?" I asked, unsure how to proceed.

"First-look. Never get sucked into an exclusive. Too restrictive," Sussman snapped, making my question seem foolish. I realized I should limit taking the lead in conversation. "Now, if you don't know it yet, I'll tell you—Eddie Upland's done. When he started giving away his tracking list, I had to cut him loose."

"Giving away his tracking list?" I said, in horror at my culpability.

"Oh, yeah, people recognized it," Jumper went on. I considered confessing to the man in order to clear Upland, but my mouth was frozen, unwilling to operate. "Truth be told, I was glad to have a reason to scalp him. It's been two years already with nothing ready to go before the camera. Pathetic. That's six months more than anybody else gives their people. What am I running here, a fucking charity?

". . . So listen, kid, Jackie's shown me some of your work. I'd seen a lot of it before, but I didn't know you had written it," he continued, allowing me to understand Eddie Upland had also been removing my name from the coverage and adding his before sending it on to Sussman. I no longer felt responsible for Upland's demise, but instead considered that justice had been done.

"It's good work. It's been very helpful. For once someone who doesn't bullshit around," Sussman finished. The words fell like benediction on me. I could no longer remember exactly when it was that I had decided to tell the truth about screenplays I'd read, even if there wasn't much truth in them. Most people out here considered telling the truth a liablility, but I had chosen to gamble and do it anyway. If I had been immersed in illegitimacy and co-opted on all other levels of the business, I had at least never compromised in this yet.

"God knows, you won't get far with that kind of honesty in this town, kid," Sussman spoke again, slapping me roughly back into reality, "but the hardest thing to find out here besides a good script, and a decent egg cream, is an opinion that's not on the fence."

"Thank you, Mr. Sussman," I said weakly.

"I don't know what'll be happening around here for a little

while, but Jackie needs help setting up the offices, and I need someone to keep reading scripts in the meantime."

"That would be terrific, Mr. Sussman," I said.

"Sure, kid. The jobs aren't growing on trees, are they?" Sussman asked with no need for a response. "And call me Jumper, even the fucking gardener does. . . . Now, where's Jackie? I have a breakfast with Kirkland and some young director they're pushing me to work with. Damn studio heads."

Jackie came back into the room shortly, decorator in tow. "Mr. Sussman, you should be off to your meeting with Mr. Kirkland, and a Mr. Glimpser," she said.

Without thinking I asked, "Paul Glimpser?"

"You know him?"

"His short was called *A Day at the Beach*," I offered.

"What'd you think?" Sussman wondered.

"Didn't like it," I said, feeling at home in my directness.

Sussman chuckled again. "Keep the frankness on our side, and you might make yourself valuable, kid. Walk with me to the dining room, tell me about this guy's film," he said, heading out.

During the walk I described Glimpser's work, and upon finishing, Sussman commented, "Sounds like crap. How's the editing?"

"Herky-jerky."

"Figures." He sighed. "Well, now all we need is someone to replace Upland. Lemme tell you why I didn't renew his contract," Sussman said. "He wanted to be a producer. To only deal with the scripts that were going to be shot." My face must have radiated perplexity. "Development fees, kid. Name of the game. Sure, I like to make the occasional movie, but that takes work. I can also set up ten to make one. Get paid for all of them. Upland never understood that," he said, shaking his head before disappearing into the executive dining room.

Sussman's words confirmed what I'd come to realize—that there were builders and there were tearers-down in this business. The writers and directors, some producers, and only a precious few studio executives were the former. The agents, along with most producers, were the latter. But then there were those who fit a separate category: they neither built nor tore down. Instead they flowed and they fed. They set up as many projects as they could, sucking in the development fees that were paid at every step of the process, with only the flimsiest of intentions to actually make most of the material they set up. While trying so hard to avoid them and become a builder, I had managed to place myself in the midst of the most nebulous of clouds, but I had now gotten nearer to the actualities of production, with this Jumper Sussman, who might or might not produce, and I wasn't about to turn back.

Temporary furniture was moved into the office space, and the phone installations were completed. I even received my own line. Jackie went about ordering office supplies that, down to the paper clip, had to be requisitioned through a lengthy system of invoices and charge numbers which were tabulated against the company's overhead allowance. Boxes arrived from the old office, and files and scripts were unloaded. Although Sussman was not seen again that week, he would soon be showing up much more regularly. Every evening for the first several days, a fresh pile of scripts under my arm, I made my way wearily home. Unable to sleep, I would get up and read until my head hurt. One night, by 5:00 A.M., I knew sleep was out of reach, so I climbed in my car and drove to the studio. I found the ledge of the reflecting pool in the shadows of the sound stages and watched the sun rise over the lot. My dreams seemed to be physically within my grasp.

Early one brutally bright morning after my custom of staying overnight at the studio had been established, I decided to launch a campaign to become known around the lot. I'd witnessed how high visibility was the real key to success at the studio. Being known for a particular attribute could be determined later, if I could make myself *known* first and foremost. I started going down each hall in the building and glad-handing any development executives, producers, assistants, even security guards and mail roomers, that I could find. It was easy to do, much easier than I had once thought. People were more friendly and willing to become acquainted with me due to my on-lot status, as well as the spate of ink the company had received in the trades regarding our move. It wasn't long before I discovered the ideal topic of conversation with my new acquaintances—box office receipts. All parties on the lot were rabid followers of this. At first I had just read the results every Monday in the trades along with everyone else; then in an extension of the focus groups that I had once directed, I started predicting the results. As I met people, I would let drop my guess on a certain film, and upon the next encounter with that person did not need to remind them what I had prognosticated.

"Nice call on that animated feature," said Chad Stillman, a marketing V.P., one Monday after I had guessed the box office within two thousand dollars.

I also became aware of the "we" phenomenon at the studio, which was rampant on the grounds from executives right on down to janitors and maintenance staff. Pictures that the studio was planning to release, that not only had I not worked on, but that I had not even seen, became "mine" too. Even past projects made and released before I had worked at the place I also claimed with "Have you seen how we did in the box office tracking?" or "We did well on our weekend release, didn't we?" or "We were certainly scotched on that per-screen average."

By a few weeks into my job, I had get-to-know-you lunches with low- to mid-echelon people scheduled through the next equinox, and was all set to head over to the Executive Building to begin my rounds there, when two of the executives actually came to me. Both men who poked their heads into my office one morning were slightly chubby, fresh-faced, almost apple-cheeked, and wore shirts and ties but no jackets, the most popular style on the lot.

"Chick Bell." The chubbier of the two introduced himself, walking into my office and extending his hand. I remembered from the trades that his father was a prominent attorney in town, and several months earlier had middle-manned a deal that put a few hundred million dollars of foreign financing into the studio's coffers. It had also resulted in Bell the younger landing a job. The other man extended a hand as well.

"Judd Atkinson," he said. "Came to welcome you aboard and see who Sussman was hiring as his new V.P."

"Nathan Pitch. You saved me a trip. I don't know the answer to your second question." I didn't recognize the man's name, and after hearing his background—corporate financial, then on staff at an entertainment newspaper—I saw him as a rare example of someone who had worked his way in on merit rather than favoritism or nepotism.

"We're on your account over at The Bunker," Bell explained, gesturing vaguely toward the tremendous building that housed the studio's executive staff and looked like something out of an Escher drawing. It had been nicknamed due to the long, airless hours the studio soldiers were required to spend there.

"Danny Halifax was going to come over with us, but Kirkland called him into a meeting. You should make a lunch with him," Bell continued. Halifax was the studio vice president in charge of servicing Iceberg's studio needs, and Kirkland was the president of the whole shooting match. He was said to be a ruthless, flamboyant, powerful, smooth, hard-driving, dynamic man. He possessed all the attributes a chief needed. In addition, he drove a domestic sports car that almost any of his employees could afford, proof of his regular guy-dom and esprit de corps. He had been in control for about sixteen months, and the first five releases made under his complete control were due out over the next two to three months. Their success would determine his fate at the studio.

Our conversation quickly ebbed when my line rang. I picked up, and a voice announced itself as "Chip, from down the hall." I had a hard time placing a face with the name, having met so many people recently, and the man asked if I could step out into the hall for a moment. His tone seemed to imply some sort of confrontation. I warily agreed and hung up.

"Gentlemen, excuse me but I have to step out and have a word with somebody," I said, getting up.

"Sure," said Atkinson.

"Do you have anything to eat in here?" Chick Bell asked. "Cookies or a piece of fruit? I'm a little hypoglycemic."

"No, we just moved in," I said, having a flash of Upland's old feeding habits, and edged toward the door.

"By the way," Bell continued, "we have a pitch meeting tomorrow. A couple of writers who are up for a project that might be right for your company. Why don't you sit in?"

"Great, I'll just clear it with Jumper," I answered.

"Eleven o'clock. Conference room seven at The Bunker."

Just then a man, a development exec from down the hall whom I had met earlier, appeared at the door.

"Hi. We were going to meet in the hall, Nathan," he said, revealing himself as the 'Chip' in question from the phone call.

"Hey, Chipper," Bell greeted him.

"Chick, Atkinson," he responded. He seemed to be very anxious as the two creative executives filed out and I followed him into the hall.

I was uneasy at first, for the man seemed a bit loose in the yolk. Chip, I recalled, had volunteered that he was a member of several twelve-step programs, and it looked like he was slipping on some of them right now as he exhorted me to hurry up. If I had only known Chip for minutes before he began talking about his past and present substance dependencies, I wondered what else he could be ready to admit after I got to know him better. Once in the hall, awash in secretaries, maintenance men, and general traffic, Chip held me up, making idle chatter, much to my confusion. Suddenly, when the hall cleared, the executive pulled me into the darkened projection booth of a screening room.

"What the . . . ?" I began, when he put his finger against my lips. Just as I was set to fly from the room, he pointed at the glazed projection window. Normally obscured by an opaque frost, there was now a half-inch square scraped clear, giving view into the screening room. There was not a screening in progress at the moment, however, but rather a body double casting session for an upcoming erotic thriller. Women, beautiful women, were standing there, and lounging, and lying flat on the floor with their arms straight back over their heads, nude, being appraised by a director and a discreet producer. For the most part they were perfect. Lovely and dark-eyed, and soft around the mouths. Their bodies were firm, an almost oil-like sheen coming off them. When they lifted their arms, the slight indentations of their ribs emerged, calling out silently through the glass. A few were a little older than the rest. They were not withered, but rather seemed a bit juiceless, their hair a texture more brittle, as their faces slowly became drawn by time. It was easy to see they wouldn't be cast. Chip excitedly recommended I watch the television screen. The only television set I could see was in the other room, barely discernible through the milky glass.

"Look up there," he directed. There was indeed another tiny pinhole scraped clear in the high right-hand corner of the window. It gave an excellent view to the television monitor playing a videotape of the session as it was recorded.

"Look at the way the camera moves over every inch of them," Chipper fairly squealed.

It was true, the camera moved with an aching slowness, devouring and then casting back every tiny bit of the bodies, from tips to toes. They were crisper, even more richly colored on the monitor than when seen directly with the eye, and that was what struck me—how much better it was to be a second-hand voyeur. Seeing their nakedness on-screen made it so much more powerful; it blunted the need for the tactile, for the actual. Feeling slightly perverse, worried about being discovered, I was nonetheless riveted—but to the monitor, not the live bodies. It was a good several minutes more before I could force myself to get back to my office. I left with a mumbled excuse, and Chip followed me back into the corridor.

"Sorry to drag you away, but I have work to do," I said.

"Don't worry about it, *amigo*," Chip said with glee. "I've been in and out of there all day."

"Well, thanks."

"Just wanted to share the wealth," Chip said, and seemed compelled by some internal force to swing an exuberant slapping handshake at me before slipping back into the projection room. I hurried back to my desk, straightening my tie and vowing to steer a wide berth of Chip. If I got pegged as that guy's friend, I would be finished.

Back in my office, my flushed face cooling back to normal, I was surprised to find a large floral arrangement waiting for me on my desk. The card read, "Best of luck in the new situation—Ronnie." I reached for the phone, but I was sure that I would be seeing her again, that it had only been a couple of weeks and I should be patient because she wanted to call the shot. I put the phone down. I had been here before, and I knew that I had to lay back, let her believe she was setting the tempo. I tried to focus on my work for the rest of the afternoon, and at last, around seven o'clock, she called.

"It occurs to me that you took my number and didn't call," she said, before I'd even said hello.

"Didn't you get my messages?"

"Unless those hang-ups on my answering machine were in Morse code, I guess not," she fired back.

"I'm not too comfortable with those machines. I don't get along that well with mine."

"Why not?" she asked.

"I don't know, it's got an attitude."

"Get a new one," she said, and then, "Meet me tonight."

"I have something after work—"

"It doesn't matter, this is a late-night place."

"Really, what do they have there?" I asked.

"They have me," she said, and I smiled. She gave me a time and directions and got off the phone saying "Ciao" and making a kissing noise that darkened the office and made it her hotel room again for just a moment before we hung up.

Later that evening I followed her directions deep into the part of the city that had once been the glamorous center of the screen trade. It was farther out than I usually went. Twenty minutes more to the east and there would no longer be any billboards in English. Twenty minutes back the way I had come, in Beverly Hills, it was as if none of this existed. This part of town had once shone but had now faded into poverty. I drove down liquid neon streets past dealers and tired professional girls out looking for a twirl, and saw the dirty squalor and the faded landmarks of Hollywood Boulevard. The stars along the sidewalk and the handprints of the famous were now scuffed over and forgotten, and I felt my chest folding up like an accordion at the sight of them. I was headed for the sagging Ashoken Hotel, where famous actors had once stayed and done legendarily scandalous things—one had even died there—but now it was an underground club.

I parked and walked toward the building, giving a thought to what might be left of my car when I returned. It was that kind of neighborhood. But I was quickly distracted. Underground clubs were a staple of the city's nightlife. They ran by word of mouth among a secret, selective network. I had never been a member, while Ronnie, it appeared, was. Usually the clubs, housed in strangely sterile banquet rooms or small, dark, hot holes, offered something that regular bars did not. Nudity, or certain sexual proclivities involving leather or foot worship, was often on the block; on other occasions, designer drugs. Most just stayed open far later than was legal. The clubs issued invitations or employed cryptic password systems governing admittance, and given these parameters, and their shrouded locations, I had never been to one.

Now, entering the ancient hotel's lobby, my heart was quick with excitement. I walked through the vaultlike entrance and up a cavernous marble staircase that led into the ballroom housing the club for tonight, or this week, or however long it would be there. The pale stone gave the underlit space a cool, museum-like feel. A threadbare tapestry ran the length of the floor, and I followed it past heavy oak and fabric chairs to a doorway blocked by several young, vibrant people in high-style clothes who crowded the door, eager to enter. Heavy bass computer-generated music pulsated from beyond them. Conversations were muffled, possibly because of the size of the place, but it sounded as if the walls were hung with wet blankets. A few tried to talk their way through the bulky doormen, who wanted none of it, but my name had been left on a list by Ronnie, and I flowed through the bottleneck. My hand was stamped with an ink that made it glow, and I stepped into the main room.

The club room was reminiscent of a marble cathedral, but the lightless air reaching toward the ceiling was filled with smoke. This room was not muffled and cool like the foyer, and the people inside were not pious worshipers. Rather, it was alive and hot, and bodies pressed together on a dance floor. They moved to two different kinds of music—the techno I had heard and also classic disco coming from separate sound systems on opposite sides of the hall—which crashed together and showered down in a cacophony. The fusion, the activity, and the humidity were causing condensation along lighting scaffolds which hung from the ceiling, and water drops were falling like noncommital rain. I stared at several seductive dancers gyrating on top of towering speakers, and then I realized they weren't dancing, but were unclothed and being painted, as they writhed, in neon colors by would-be artists kneeling at their feet.

The room smelled like perfume-sweat and cloves and camphor, and made me want to find Ronnie and dance with abandon. I looked for the bar, where I was to meet her, and where I would have to have a drink, or several, to reach the place these people inhabited. Spotting the bar across the room, I threaded my way through revelers and chairs as I advanced toward it. I ordered a drink, and just as the bartender delivered, I felt a pair of soft, cool hands cover my eyes. I made a pretense of feeling her rings before yelling above the din, "Veronica Sylvan?" She spun me around and kissed me, spun me around again and led me after her.

"Leave that," she said, gesturing to my drink.

The way she guided me across the floor made me feel like I was at the end of a stunted conga line, and my shouts of "How are you?" and "Where are we going?" went unheard or unheeded by her. We finally arrived at a passageway that looked like it led to the kitchen, but was blocked by a short velvet rope between two brass posts, and a large man wearing an earpiece and microphone. He raised a handheld ultraviolet light at us, but seeing Ronnie, he lowered it, unclipped the rope, and moved it aside. I mumbled thanks and Ronnie dragged me, not into a kitchen, but rather a small sitting room populated by a number of thin, impossibly attractive women and a few heavy, but very tan, men. One of the men, mustachioed and dressed like an Edwardian, I recognized as a producer of sexual thrillers that were constantly surrounded by rumors of his on-set perversion. Everyone in the room was sprawled lethargically on plumply stuffed couches, and though seeing was difficult due to the stygian atmosphere, I made out several bottles of greenish liquid, and several more bell-shaped glasses, littering the small tables in front of us.

"Care for an absinthe, dear?" Ronnie asked. My eyes adjusted to the dark, and I looked at her. She was stunning and a little outrageous in a crushed velvet cloche and a man's cut suit of dark silk that draped open, showing her black lace bra.

"Absinthe," I repeated. After witnessing it at several functions, I had done some research and knew it had disappeared early in the century through a combination of laws and intolerance. "I thought the stuff makes you insane?" I asked, communicating a fact I had learned.

"Only when it contains too much wormwood, friend," a refined but obese man spoke from across the room. "Wormwood is the root that gives absinthe potency. Without wormwood you are drinking mere pastis."

Ronnie placed a glass in my hand and directed me to a sofa. "Sit," she said.

"So is there wormwood in this variety? How do we know if it contains too much?" I asked.

"Don't be silly, darling, the wormwood is what makes it

what it is. But this batch has the right amount," she said, pouring a small splash of the green liquid into each of our glasses. She then laid a silver strainer-type spoon shaped like the Eiffel Tower across each, rested a few sugar cubes on top of them, and began trickling water over the apparatus and into the glasses. Witnessing the process, I remembered the people with the teacups and flask at Asylum the night we had met.

"All these people?" I asked, gesturing out toward the main room of the club.

"Some. Some are on cocaine or other drugs. Some are just drunk. Some are sober. What's the difference?" she said, removing the strainers and stirring the sodden sugar cubes into the mixture, which was now turning a cloudy whitish-green.

"No difference." I shrugged, accepting the glass she offered.

She raised hers and we touched rims. I paused for a moment, breathing deeply, but knew that I was going ahead and saw no sense in waiting. I drank a healthy slug, draining half the glass. It was faintly licorice-tasting and refreshing, not minty, though, as I expected due to the color. It was cold too, from the water, I supposed.

"Do you like?" Ronnie asked, curling into me.

"I think so," I said, swallowing the rest, feeling its tendrils reach out into my blood.

As if from a great distance I heard the mustachioed man say to somebody, "Yes. *Chernobyl.* That's the word for wormwood in the Russian tongue. The coincidence is quite devastating, no?" I realized he was talking to me when he clapped me warmly on the shoulder.

"This stuff could bring back the days of ennui," I mused

lazily, now knowing why all in the room were laid out like so on the couches.

"No, my good man, ennui is passé," said the mustachioed man on his way out of the room. "These are the days of fear. Strictly fear." I shuddered and drank again.

As the night wore on, and the absinthe flowed, I began to feel a sensation of forgetfulness take hold of me. I briefly fought to recall something that Oscar Wilde had said about absinthe. *The first stage is like ordinary drinking, the second when you begin to see monstrous and cruel things, but if you can persevere, you will enter upon the third stage, where you see things that you want to see, wonderful curious things....* But his words melted away, as did the sucking gravity-like feeling that had once trapped my feet and held them to the earth.

The usual exhaustion and incoherence that accompanied heavy drinking was far off as Ronnie continued to pour. She moved closer to me too with each glass, and soon it was as if we were communicating deeply with each other although neither of us spoke. Others in the room began to drift away. I did not witness them walk out, but suddenly they were no longer present. All at once Ronnie and I were alone in the room, except for the cozy velvet furniture, and then we were all over each other. Our hungry mouths found fabric, then flesh as we grappled blindly. My equilibrium left me as I entered her. I felt I was mounting boundless horizons, tumbling through an ocean of green alluvium, then went on into blackness.

Returning to sentience much later, I was disappointed to

find her gone. I rubbed my eyes and peered around the room, discovering I was completely alone. I had a brief moment when I felt the same accordion-like feeling in my chest that I had earlier, but I tucked my shirt in, drew myself back together, and gave myself a sprinkle in the face from one of the leftover water decanters. I checked my watch and found it was past four o'clock, but amazingly the music still pumped relentlessly outside. Walking back out into the slightly less populated club, I began to look for her.

A quarter hour elapsed, and after wading through the crowd of dwindling revelers, I was still empty-handed. My spirits began to sink along with my hopes of finding her as the absinthe faded, and I realized I was utterly alone. I located a pay phone and dialed Ronnie's number, only to reach her answering machine. I swore the filthy machine was against me. With no sign of her, or any of the others from the private room, and still a little lit from the strange head the absinthe brought, I went to my car. Upon finding it intact, I headed for home.

Along the way, fighting to stay focused, I finally recalled what Oscar Wilde had said of absinthe. I had gotten it slightly wrong the first time, I supposed, because I was already well past the fourth glass when I had thought of it, but now his words reverberated in me. *After the first glass you see things as you wish they were. After the second, you see things as they are not. Finally you see things as they really are, and that is the most horrible thing in the world. . . .*

As I drove back from the depths of the city and crossed the cement river that held no water, as I passed beneath the sad palms that hung their heads along my way home, as I went through the green stoplights that echoed the color of the drink and the empty streets that made it seem I was on a movie set—I saw my situation clearly for the first time. I neared my neighborhood, and the towers of Century City hunched over me like a pair of menacing bullies. I took the ramp up to Avenue of the Stars. I wound around the circular bend and wished the ramp just kept going up, because I wanted to go to the stars. I wanted to drive up into the black night between the towers and disappear amongst them. To detach from my job, the filthy city, and the planet. To move freely through space. But when I reached the top of the ramp, there were no stars visible there. The bright haze of the city at night makes them invisible. No, there was just more glittering road and streetlights lining the way toward my apartment.

CHAPTER SEVEN

The next morning, before I had absorbed what I had experienced, even before I had consoled myself for my tremendous hangover, I saw Eddie Upland's face. The trades were lying on my desk when I walked in, and on the front page of one there was a small photo of him, smiling, under a blurb announcing, "Upland Ankles Iceberg, Named New Prexy of Concerto Pics." Reading the item, I learned that the deposed executive had landed like a cat and was now in charge of a film company that, contrary to what its name implied, specialized in low-budget martial arts features that sold to a large foreign market and did a brisk video business. There was no other field where one could fail upward so rapidly, except perhaps politics. I didn't begrudge Upland his good fortune either, figuring that soon enough he would be a bust at his new job as well, and then get his own production deal at a studio in reward. It would be helpful to be on his good side then, so I wrote his name on my call sheet to offer my congratulations. Picking up the trades, I walked over to Sussman's office to see if he was in and had read the article.

Jackie was dug in behind her crowded desk, dealing with a battery of phones when I walked in. Her well-dyed blond hair had grown a dirty shade within the past weeks, due to a lack of time for touch-ups, I surmised. Her office, though, adjoining Sussman's, had gone a long way toward being furnished during this period of time. It had forsaken its bareness for poor taste in decorating. Sussman's wife had gone wild buying objets d'art, and the result was a ghastly melange of pop-art statues fashioned from metal and cardboard, abstract modern canvases that looked like vomited paint, and dark-hued Art Deco furniture that drew in and imprisoned the light and air of the room. Jackie didn't look happy, and the art might have had something to do with this. I held up the paper in front of her, pointing at Upland's picture, and she nodded, finally disengaging herself from a call.

"Is he actually in?" I asked, signaling toward Sussman's closed door.

"He's on with his wife. Yelling at her about the furniture bill. He said you should go on in." Jackie sighed.

I took a deep breath, wishing I'd had a cup of coffee. My heart was thudding, and blood rambled around my temples. My stomach had just bottomed out too, and for an instant I felt like I was going to die, but then it passed, though I knew it would happen again if I didn't get something to eat or drink. I tapped twice against the producer's door and stepped in.

Sussman looked up and waved for me to take a seat, which I did gratefully.

"Listen, honey, you did a great job, I just think any more procuring for this place and we're going to have a permanent collection," Sussman said to his wife over the telephone. I looked around and decided that if Jackie's office had been overdone, Sussman's was even more excessive. Slabs of marble and metal made up coffee table/sculptures; chairs like the one I sat down on littered the room and were pleasant to neither ass nor eye, and the walls held tableaus bearing color schemes straight out of a migraine headache.

"Dear, my meeting just walked in." Sussman rolled his eyes. "Yes, Nathan Pitch, my development guy."

I fiddled briefly with an exquisitely lacquered humidor on the desk in front of me, the only really fetching piece in the room, and then caught myself and stopped immediately.

"Yes, dear, I'll ask him," and then, "We could open an exhibit here, though. All right? I'll talk to you soon." Sussman hung up and turned toward me. "The studio gives me an unlimited budget to do my offices, and my wife exceeds it."

I nodded my understanding.

"My wife would like you to take a look at a project for her," Sussman said.

"Did she write it?"

"Nah. Her manicurist or yoga instructor. Some damn thing." Sussman sighed.

"Sure," I answered. I had heard that Naomi Sussman considered anybody who worked for her husband as working for her as well, and I feared this might be the start of some ugly terrain.

"You married, Nathan?" Sussman asked.

"No, Jumper," I answered, feeling as if my wheels were about to fall off.

The producer cocked his head back for a moment, as if insulted, but then seemed to remember he'd told me to go ahead and use the moniker. "You look like shit, kid. You feel okay?"

Before I could answer, the intercom sounded and Jackie's voice came through. "Doug Kirkland on three," she said.

"All right," Jumper said, reaching for the phone. I half got up and motioned maybe I should step out, it being the studio head on the phone and all. Sussman waved me back into my chair and put a finger to his lips. Pressing the speaker button on the phone, he began, "Doug. How are you?"

Across the way in his architecturally fortified mausoleum, The Bunker, Kirkland spoke. "Let's talk about the Patrick Hackman project."

"I had a great two-hour meeting with him," Sussman said, flipping up the lid on his humidor and inhaling.

"I know, I know. I heard you had this terrific, like three-hour-long meeting with him. He loves you," the studio chief responded.

"He's a terrific guy. What a meeting." Jumper eyed his cigars, resting in brown, even rows.

"What do you think of the project?" Kirkland wondered.

"Needs a lot of work," Sussman said. "What do you think?"

"I see this as a smash. Its potential is phenomenal. Though

it's all over the place now, I've seen moments in this guy's writing as deep and focused as any I've read," Kirkland said passionately.

"The meeting with this guy went so well, it went on for four hours."

"We need a producer like you to work with the guy. To elevate this piece," Kirkland said.

Sussman leaned back with a dull glaze of satisfaction in his eyes, and with wet, rubbery lips he said, "Yes, there's real potential here. The meeting went so well, he's probably *still* at my house."

"We need you!" Kirkland stressed.

"It does sound like a winner. I'll do it," Sussman decided and hung up with an almost postcoital glow. The way they spoke was as if the truth slipping in anywhere along the assembly line might cause the entire garish, bunker-like executive building and the studio itself to creak and groan and tumble to the ground, and they were guarding against this so the whole damn structure was earthquake-proof.

"Listen, Nathan, I want to go over some things with you later on today. Free up some time this afternoon," Sussman said, all business again.

I nodded resignedly. "I was invited to a meeting by Bell and Atkinson. I wanted to clear it with you," I volunteered.

"What kind of meeting?" Sussman asked snappily, as if he were all of a sudden seated atop a perch far above the office.

"Some writers are pitching a comedy. The studio might want you to produce it," I said, wondering if I was going to be cuffed back into place for this.

"Check it out. Can't hurt," Sussman said imperiously, letting me know just what kind of magnanimity I was being shown. Then in a tone that let me see exactly how things stood: "Come see me and tell me every detail this afternoon. Set up our appointment through Jackie."

"Yes, sir," I said, and got up. As I did, the office door opened, and two deliverymen dollied in a high-tech exercise bicycle. Jackie, hustling in behind them, directed its placement in the corner.

"Great, that's just what I need," Sussman said as I strode out, hoping I didn't appear as shaky as I felt.

Walking across the lot to The Bunker for my meeting, I stopped at the commissary for coffee. I tried to pick myself up by continuing my meeting-and-greeting regimen with people I stood next to in line. It wasn't really working, though, as all I had on my mind was going back to bed, and Ronnie, and a thought or two of the lovely green absinthe. I bolted down the inky coffee forcefully, wishing it was a dram of absinthe. Though it was morning, I felt a strange itch for another taste of it. I drew on fading discipline to drag myself to the appointed conference room where I found Bell and Atkinson awaiting me. The two creative executives were immersed in discussion over photocopied reviews of a play they had spread before them. Bell was trying to make a point to an unconvinced Atkinson.

"I'm telling you, this could be giant," he said.

"I just don't think it translates to the screen." Atkinson sighed.

I caught a look at the review they swept away upon my arrival. Originally the story had been a classic American novel, which had already been successfully translated into a classic, multi-award–winning film, and had now recently been revived as a notice-gathering Broadway production. Bell abandoned the secrecy and held up the review for me to see, earnestly inquiring, "Is there a movie in this or what?"

"Uh, yeah, Chick, it's already been made," I pointed out.

Bell covered his gaff without missing a beat. "Of course, I'm talking about a remake."

"You don't look too good, Pitch," Atkinson said by way of changing the subject.

I shrugged and said nothing, feeling suddenly overcome by a sense of fragility. I thought it too must be a result of the absinthe, and wished I could wrap myself up in tissue paper to protect my senses, which were registering stimulae too finely.

"I use this stuff called bronze extender. It gives you a little healthy color," Bell offered helpfully.

"I'll get to the beach this weekend," I said, speaking their language, and before long the two writers showed up to tell us their story.

The writers, Mittman and McCullough, were a team known for their facility with comedy. Before I had arrived in town, I had thought writing a solitary profession, something done in quiet. But no, here it was done two and three at a time, aloud, and with great festivity. The pair were difficult to tell apart. Both had slightly unkempt collar-length hair, loose, unironed shirts, faded jeans, and leather cases slung over their shoulders. Both took out notes and put on wire-rimmed spectacles and began the pitch, one keeping the ball rolling, the momentum flowing, and the other gauging reactions, nipping a word here, tucking a point there, tailoring the story to what they imagined were our specifications.

They were in to tell a down-to-earth, romantic family comedy about a career bachelor who is forced to baby-sit a beautiful young single mother's kids. The writers needed to create a believable setup, likable characters, an element of romance between the bachelor and the mother, and let the high jinks and hilarity ensue. The movie was supposed be a cute piece of summer fare, but soon after they began, Mittman and McCullough spun off course. I realized that they were missing the point of what the studio was looking for when they started talking about a plot of political intrigue that the family got mixed up in. I got the impression that they weren't actually writers but vaudevillians as they kept their plots spinning like plates on sticks. I began to tune out and lose them as their main characters arrived in Washington, D.C., where they took part in a transvestite parade and thwarted an attempt to assassinate the premier of China, and only came to my senses again as I watched the studio executives' heads bob slavishly, laughing like puppets at one implausible setup after the next that led to the climax.

I realized a grave shortcoming of mine was that I lacked a convincing fake laugh. A big, hearty, guffawing chuckle, often employed, that called for those ever present fleshy lips to pull back, exposing dripping teeth. One that jiggled the jowls perversely. I certainly could have used one in this meeting.

"I like it. I like it very much," Bell said repeatedly, Atkinson concurring. I could not believe this, and I looked at the creative executives incredulously.

I certainly couldn't agree, venturing a "I'm not sure the boss will go for it, but I'll be in touch."

As the writers left, before I had even turned toward the two creative executives, Bell finally stated the obvious: "Well, that was terrible." But somewhere down the road Mittman and McCullough might do something viable and remember Bell and Atkinson as fans. I slackened inside as I realized I would certainly not be viewed as a friendly audience in the future.

As we checked the writers' list, conferring on other choices for the project, the laughter over how bad Mittman and McCullough had been dwindled. What replaced it was a sort of confusion that covered the studio execs' faces like shrouds. Everyone here knew that lying to others was par for the course, and deceiving oneself was fine as well. It was only when one forgot to remember that one was deceiving oneself that one became lost. When even the nature of the lie and the essence of the truth slipped away, one relinquished all claims on humanity and became a roving predator, not just an animal hunting for food—not even a shark cruising on instinct alone—but a filthy, snapping hyena, foraging for refuse. This was the current countenance Bell and Atkinson wore. I was amazed that the word creative was used in connection with their job titles at all.

Arriving back in my office, I saw with dismay that while I had been at the meeting, a daunting, eye-wrecking pile of scripts had accumulated on my desk. Despite the flashing light on my voice mail, I waded into the material and began reading. At this level of the business, I was now finally looking at serious projects. The scripts that would be selling for big dollars, written by established writers for money, not by those merely scrapping for representation. For my own edification I had begun to read some screenplays the studio had bought and put into production. Million- and multimillion-dollar script purchases I had previously been learning about only from the trades.

Late in the day I arrived at one in particular, an action-buddy script that had been penned by a young writer named Terry Mauve, who had already written several hit movies following a similar formula. As much as I wanted to dismiss it, as I read the first twenty pages I had to admit the screenplay was very gripping. I read on, and was on the verge of truly caring about one of the characters when it seemed Mauve just quit. There was a love scene about halfway through the script, and instead of actually writing it, the screenwriter had merely penned, "Insert the steamiest sex scene you ever imagined right here." It was clever. It was cheeky. It probably sent ripples of admiration through the entire community, but it went too far for me to tolerate in my post-absinthe state. Sure, love scenes were ultimately choreographed by the director, but this guy had been paid millions for something he had only alluded to instead of written. Without further thought I opened a document on my computer and typed "Untitled" where the title should be, and underneath it, "A screenplay by Terry Mauve." On the next page I typed:

FADE IN:

A black wiseass cop and a tough white cop who don't
like each other are teamed up. Insert movie here.

I printed this out and put another hundred pages of blank,
three-hole punch paper behind it, put FADE OUT on the last
page, attached the title sheet, and bound it in a script cover.
I quickly wrote up an anonymous copy-request form and a
distribution memo to the studio's "Creative Group." It meant
that the script would be photocopied and sent to all the executives as a new project for the evening read. It was going
to cause a stir, and if I was discovered to be behind it, I was
certain to be fired. But I just didn't care. It was either this or
go into the men's room, kneel, and vomit up all the hypocrisy
I had suddenly become so keenly aware of. After I sent away
the package through inter-office mail, I walked into Jackie's
office and canceled my meeting with Sussman.

"He's going to be angry," she warned.

"Who's he in there with? I'll tell him myself," I said, leaning over and reading Jumper's schedule.

"He's interviewing someone for the vice-president position.
He won't be able to reschedule with you until next week,"
Jackie said, covering the appointment book, but exposing
Sussman's call sheet. Upside down, I could still read it. I had
at least learned this much from my agency days. I clearly saw
Ronnie Sylvan's name on the call sheet. I wasn't sure what it
meant. It might be legitimate business, but could it be a call
regarding me?

"I'm going home sick," I said, meaning it. On my way out, I stopped in my office to retrieve my messages. The voice mail played Ronnie Sylvan's melodious voice: "Don't you know you're supposed to call the day after?" and she'd left a mobile phone number. I halfheartedly dialed the number, and Ronnie picked up through a crackle of static.

"Where'd you run off to?" she said, in her classic style of reversal that few people probably bothered questioning.

"I guess I just had to go," I answered, not one of those few.

"When are we going to see each other again?" she asked.

"Soon?"

"Promise me Saturday night week after next. I have something good for us," she demanded. "But we'll also get together before that."

"Sure," I said.

"Has Sussman done anything about the veepee job?" she asked, the static getting worse. I was quickly covered by a new wave of sickness. I was being worked, worked for something I did not have to offer. Before I could answer, she said, "I'm going into the canyon—" and the call was abruptly cut off. It seemed even the landscape was working in collusion with her. I put a few scripts under my arm and left the lot as quickly as possible. To stay for another moment, I feared, would cause me to fulfill the vision of myself kneeling on the tiled men's room floor.

As I left the lot, I tried to understand what had overcome me. I was no longer a stranger to a formidable hangover, nor

was I innocent to the ordure of the business, but today I had
been as vulnerable to both as a patch of raw skin to a steel
brush. Perhaps I was looking for some connection to this
quicksilver woman I had spent two nights with. Perhaps it was
directly related to the mysterious compound I had drunk. I
felt an odd tingling in my limbs, and the road in front of me
became an oily smear. I pulled over into the breakdown lane
and wiped a greasy coating of sweat from the back of my neck.
While this was usually the moment I promised myself not to
drink again on regular day-afters, today I had a sudden and
dire need for more of what I'd had the night before. It wasn't
a thirst exactly, but a painful, involuntary contraction deep
inside me that I seemed to know on a cellular level only absinthe would soothe. I guided my car back onto the road. I
drove past dusty fields of phallic oil derricks over the hill and
toward the Ashoken Hotel. I noticed everything was built ugly
and cheap along the roadsides as I neared it. There were chain
stores selling forty types of chicken and video stores pumping
out the offerings we pumped out first up at the studios. Every
place else, it seemed, distributed money from machines, or
sold beer, or both.

I located the club and stomped up the threadbare carpeted
steps two at a time. No music emanated from the main room
now; instead there were the banging sounds of carpentry. I
walked in and saw a maintenance crew of sorts dismantling
the club apparatus—the lighting scaffolds, the speakers, the
dancing platforms. I approached one of the workers who was
stacking wares into boxes behind the makeshift bar.

"You shouldn't be in here," the man said brusquely.

"Yeah," I answered, "but can you tell me when this place will be open again?"

"Don't know," the man said, continuing his work.

"Don't know or won't say?" I wondered aloud. The man did not respond.

"Listen, I want a bottle of absinthe," I said straight out.

"I don't know what that is, and besides, it would be very expensive." The man shrugged.

"What've you got?" I went ahead and pulled out my wallet. The man moved aside one of the cartons and produced a full-sized fifth bottle, and another small-sized one, about a pint, nearly full.

"This seems to be all that's left," the man said, holding his arms around them protectively.

"How much?" I asked, opening my wallet wide. Rather than give me an answer, the man simply kept nodding as I pulled out bills, and finally folded up the wad and went back to boxing the bar utensils. I removed my jacket, wrapped my new purchases in it, and left. On the way to the car I took a nip from the small, opened bottle. It was more bitter than I remembered, and I decided I must wait until I got home to cut it with sugar and water.

I reached home to find a mountainous pile of laundry had slowly annexed my living space. I drained a glass of absinthe and, as if I'd taken a tonic, immediately felt myself again. So energized, I set about gathering my clothes. The laundry room, usually a cool and comfortable cave bathed in tubal fluorescent rays, was no respite for me today. This was due to the strobe-like effect caused by a failing bulb. It gave the room the look of a Genet play put on in a Soho repertory theater, and after starting the wash I hurriedly returned to my apartment, where I drank several more glasses before falling into a hollow state that vaguely resembled sleep.

When I arose the next morning, before leaving for work, I went down to the laundry room and saw that the lid to the machine I had used was open. I found it invasive to have my things moved, but it was my fault this time for leaving my clothes in the machine for so long. I opened the dryer, where I suspected my clothes had been moved, but all the dryers were empty as well. My clothes were gone. My very clothes, stolen. Who could it have been? I didn't know anybody in my building to choose as a suspect. My circuits seemed to just jam, and the situation made me laugh. Quietly at first, and then with more gusto. My laughter echoed off the laundry room's cinder-block walls to the accompaniment of the wildly flickering light.

As I returned from work at increasingly late hours each day now, my evening routine became a cycle of preparing and imbibing several welcoming glasses of absinthe. I went through the fifth within several days, keeping the smaller bottle in my car as a souvenir, a talisman. Returning to the club site six days in a row, I found it alive again one night and purchased a few more bottles. The amount of cash I had laid out should have concerned me, but the drink didn't seem to affect me adversely otherwise. Morning aftereffects were no longer noticeable. On the contrary, I was reading more scripts than ever, several per day—hundreds and hundreds of pages—to the point where I had to squint to see in the distance and began to suffer eye strain. I tried to continue meeting people and generally make myself useful. In fact, the prospect of a few nighttime cordials helped me square away my work more rapidly, so that I could head for home and drift away.

One night in particular I lost a little track of myself and indulged in several more glasses than usual. Much to my surprise the next morning, rather than awakening with a headache, I awoke with a light heart. On my way to the office one of the studio security guards that I had made the acquaintance of stopped me.

"Mr. Pitch," he said, "my buddy on the night shift and me wrote a screenplay. You want to take a look at it?"

"Is it about some night security guards at a movie studio?" I asked, full of smiles.

"Yeah, they make a movie at night, secretly, and it's a big hit and it saves the studio," the man answered intently.

"Movies about movies are a tough sell. Change it to some other kind of corporation. Big business. Have them save the company. Send it over when you're finished," I said, and walked on.

Strolling into Jackie's office, I got the news that Jumper was on his way to a meeting in the bunker with Danny Halifax, a studio vice president. "You're supposed to meet him there, to discuss re-writers on that action project," she said.

"Sure thing," I responded, and prepared to head over when I noticed the blond had all but totally bled out of Jackie's hair. In addition, her face was drawn and exhausted. I saw how the job was beginning to eat her up, just as it had been doing to me only a short time ago, before I had gotten things in hand.

The meeting with the V.P. was slated for nine o'clock, and was to last for an hour. We were going to discuss writers for an upcoming action film about a rogue corps of Marines and talk about the Patrick Hackman script as well. Writers in town were very specialized, and different ones were brought in for different purposes. Some handled jokes, some action sequences, some pathos, some charm, and yet others body parts. My comprehensive knowledge of these writers and their specialties was why I was to be in the meeting. Sussman was being driven to the lot and would meet me at The Bunker. Just before I left, Jackie's phone rang. It was Halifax's office. The veep was running late, and we were told to show up at nine fifteen. No problem for Sussman, there was traffic in the canyon anyway.

Upon arriving at the appointed 9:15, I was kept waiting in the vestibule until 9:25. I heard Halifax continuing his calls inside. It was obvious he wasn't going to stop until Sussman got there. Minutes later, the producer arrived, nodded to me with a certain amount of disdain, and we were shown in.

All were seated by nine thirty, but Halifax's assistant poked his head in to announce an incoming telephone call of much importance. Halifax, crisply done up from his razor-cut hair to his starchy shirt and knife-like pleated slacks, flung a pencil toward the door at the invading head. The head ducked and pulled back, and the pencil sailed high. The casual hostility of the gesture struck me as familiar. Nonetheless, Halifax dashed out and took a quick private call on his minion's phone, leaving Sussman and I sitting looking at each other.

At nine thirty-five Halifax sat down behind his desk again, and read aloud a short item from a trade paper slandering the studio for several financial indiscretions by the brass involving the studio's corporate jet, as well as a larcenous run of box office failures. Chortling about the effect it would have on morale, he picked up his phone and made a prank call to Atkinson, who had previously worked at the particular trade. There was a suspicious volume of solid information in the article, and Atkinson was thought to be the leak. Halifax left word that he was the paper calling to verify the quotes, and hung up chuckling. Jumper laughed heartily as well. Feeling in good humor, I decided if I couldn't beat them, I would certainly join them, that today I would unveil my own laugh. I let go with my new counterfeit snigger. These executive types were always snorting and slobbering all over themselves with mirth, so I did too, without self-consciousness. Halifax, possibly offended deep into his burnished studio roots, looked surprised at my outburst, which by virtue of its duration *was* becoming a bit inappropriate. He fell silent.

Sussman turned toward me and said in a surly tone, "You don't pack enough rank to laugh at that," but this only seemed to fuel my humor for a moment until I got it back under control.

At nine forty-five the slick-smooth veep got up with a baseball bat, a Louisville Slugger with his own name custom-burned into the barrel, and began taking cuts at the air as he fired off writers' names for consideration. "Cramb and Scaranov," he said of a team that had just booked a long television deal.

"Unavailable," I informed. "Wolfe and Greenburger, though," I said, throwing out the names of a top character-drama team. "Or what about Chris Staley?" I said of a top body-count man. As I would mention a name, Halifax would gloss by it as if he hadn't heard a sound.

"You know what I'm thinking?" Halifax paused for emphasis not two minutes later. "Greenburger and Wolfe." I was incredulous as Sussman nodded in agreement. All the while Halifax swung his bat viciously. Once again there was something familiar about the manner in which he was swiping at the air with his bat. Halifax continued to name people from the writers list that sat on his desk who were unacceptable, overpriced, or dead. He named people his sister went to school with, and with whom we should "take a meeting." (When I called him back the next day and asked if he would hire these people, he answered either "Of course not" or "I never suggested that.")

Checking his watch at 9:50, the V.P. put down his bat, ruffled his hair, and said, "Good. Let's get going on this. It's theeee . . . sixteenth. Let's meet again on the thirtieth and have the list down to Greenburger and Wolfe and three other names from which to make a final decision. By then we'll have another draft of the Hackman script to go over too."

Then, to my bewilderment, he headed for the door saying, "If you'll excuse me, I have a staff meeting in Kirkland's office." It didn't seem to bother Sussman, who already appeared quite bored with the proceedings. Again, something about the way he excused himself made me finally put together what I found familiar about Halifax.

"Danny," I asked, "where were you before you started with the studio?"

"I was director of development for a small independant company," he answered as he slipped on an extremely well-tailored suit jacket.

"And before that?" I pressed.

"I was on Mickey Kessler's desk at the big agency," he answered.

"I see," I said. "So was I. How did you get on his desk?"

Jumper was looking at the two of us strangely, but didn't interrupt as Halifax answered uncomfortably, "Out of the mail-room. You?"

"Same," I said. We shared what could only be described as a potent look of intimacy, and I understood that the baseball bat was this man's version of the famous Kessler bullwhip. He had learned much from our old teacher. Then I had a flash of a younger Halifax in the L'Ermitage, like a deer caught in the headlights of an oncoming truck, ready to do his duty for Mrs. Kessler. The image nearly made me burst out laughing once again. Only the stern look coming from Sussman kept me relatively poker-faced. In another moment Danny Halifax was gone. We were left sitting in his office feeling like we had been serviced by a high-priced hooker—spent and a little dirty from only five minutes of action for our hour's worth of time.

Walking back to our offices, Jumper stopped and turned to me. "Here comes my dressing-down," I thought with an un-diminished amount of levity.

"Reschedule that meeting of ours with Jackie for next week," he said. "And from now on, I'll tell you when you leave sick."

I bit the inside of my cheek to maintain my serious face.

"And never pin a guy down like that," he continued. "That's what lawyers and agents are for."

"But—" I began.

"No. Everyone here knows all about Mickey Kessler and his wife. My real name is Arnold, but everybody calls me Jumper. In this town we can be anyone we want to be, because we let each other." As I stood there in the midst of the lot and business went on around us, I saw it unfiltered and unadulterated for the first time: the truth was of no account here, fact was fiction by design.

"Leave lunch open next Monday. I want you to meet the new vice president I hired." The producer turned and started walking again at a pace that left no doubt I was not invited to follow.

CHAPTER EIGHT

Several days later I was stepping back into my office after a meeting and was surprised to see Ronnie Sylvan sitting behind my desk. She had her feet up, a high-heeled pump dangling indolently from one toe. On the desktop, next to my ever present towers of scripts, rested a gift box from an expensive clothing store. "Can I fuck you for lunch?" she asked. It was a straightforward query, but the way she said it made me wonder at the dreams of independence she had been brought up on, as if being able to ask such questions with assurance proved she was in charge of her destiny.

"I might be able to get away," I answered, thinking about the small bottle of absinthe in my drawer and her feline presence behind my desk.

"Good."

I wondered how she had gotten on the lot without a pass,

but realized the security guards were no match for her. I sat down in my own guest chair across from her.

"For you," she said, sliding the box toward me with a sheer-stockinged foot, uncrossing her legs in the process and giving me an indecorous look past her silk garters and up her skirt.

"Thanks," I said, opening the box. Inside were a blindingly white linen shirt and an elegant dark silk tie, as well as a pair of navy silk boxer shorts, all by Forrenti. They weren't really my style, by virtue of their price. I knew these items alone cost twice what I had extravagantly paid for the absinthe awhile back. "Lovely."

"Shall we go?" she asked.

"How about the executive dining room?"

"Boring," was her response. I named another nearby choice, King Dragon, and before we left, I slipped the small bottle of absinthe into my jacket pocket.

As we reached the door she said, "So what's going on with the V.P. job?" Though I knew someone had been hired, I figured I would play out the charade.

"Not sure," I said.

"How about putting in a word for someone with Jumper for me?" She smiled sweetly.

"Come to think of it, I believe someone has been hired," I said, wanting to leave and not reveal my lack of entrée with Sussman. But my answer caused that smile of hers to vanish like a rabbit into a hedgerow. "I heard a certain influential writer is up in arms over a mock script that went around with his name on it," she said casually.

"Really? What's it called?" I asked.

"It was untitled apparently. You wouldn't know anything about it, I suppose?" she asked.

"No," I said, "but I'll let you know if I hear anything. I had a meeting with Halifax the other day, and he didn't mention it."

"That's because he doesn't read anything. But you read everything, so I was sure you'd know about it."

"Well, maybe it's too late," I said, understanding her message, "but I guess I could weigh in with an endorsement for someone."

She smiled. It was the ticket. "Kathleen Sanger. A good friend. She's met with Jumper, and she'll certainly do a great job."

"Wait here," I said, and walked into Jackie's office.

"I'm going to lunch, Jackie," was all I told her.

"Okay, Nathan."

"Nice blouse. Nice earrings."

"Thanks and thanks." I left and rejoined Ronnie.

"Done," I said. "Let's go."

We were seated quickly at King Dragon, an upscale Chinese eatery that was known for its excellent food in this town, but would have been out of business in a month back in New York, where there were real restaurants. It was crowded, and only Ronnie's way with the maître d' got us a table without a long wait. Every seat was occupied by well-dressed studio types, filling me with a moment's regret over my choice. Between the two of us, we waved hello to nearly everyone in the place. She went on to more elaborate greetings with some people, air-kissing them on both cheeks. The hyena boys,

Chick Bell, Atkinson, nutty Chipper, were all there, and even Kirkland was seated in a corner with a plump elderly man. I took in the scene—all of us executives out for lunch in our shirts and ties. We who thought we were so smart and mobile, but who were really prisoners on furlough. The ties we wore around our necks were literally leashes. Kessler had been doing Feller a favor when he had snipped off the kid's tie. He had been cutting him loose, but Feller had been too stupid to see it, and so had I.

"Kind of high-profile." I grimaced, shaking the image from my head.

"Isn't it . . ." Ronnie smiled, waving at someone over my shoulder.

"Who's that Kirkland's with?"

"You don't recognize Lubin?" she said as if it were obvious. It was true, I should have known the CEO of the multinational company that owned the studio. Lubin was Kirkland's boss. Every one of these power guys, from Bell to Halifax, to Kirkland, to Lubin, right on up, all acted like they were some sort of king, but the truth was that every one of them answered to somebody. Just as Sussman was subordinate to Kirkland, Kirkland bowed to the CEO, Lubin. Lubin, in turn, knelt before the chairman of the studio's parent company, and the chairman was controlled by the board, which was directed by the shareholders. These executives wielded their power convincingly enough, but at the core it was a sham. They would all be fired sooner than later and live in fear of that until it happened.

A waiter approached, and I requested two glasses of water.

"Leave the teacups please. And some sugar." A suspicious glint came to Ronnie's eye, and I clandestinely showed her the small bottle I had in my jacket.

"A visit with the green fairy during the day? You're a bad boy," she whispered. I shrugged and poured a splash in each cup. The small bottle had a sticker with the symbol 70° on it, which meant seventy percent alcohol. One hundred-forty proof.

"Where'd you get that?" she asked.

"Bought it back at the club."

"Bought it?" she said.

"Yeah. It was pricy too."

"You don't have to pay for it, silly. Just Taft-Hartley a bouncer or a bartender, they'll give you whatever you want."

"Taft-Hartley" was industry jargon for the Screen Actors Guild regulation that required an actor to be in a film before being eligible for membership. But membership was required before being hired for a union film, so it presented quite a hurdle. By putting a non-union actor into a film as an extra or a walk-through, and having the company pay the fee for his Screen Actors Guild card, one was doing an unparalleled favor for a new actor. "I don't have that power," I allowed.

"Just tell them you do. Make them believe it. They'll want to . . . False sincerity is only one key to this town," she said definitively, before we poured more drinks and went on with our meal.

Later on, when lunch had extended to a room in the Starlite Inn, she leaned back and commented, "I give great head, don't I?"

"I could say I've had better—"

"But you'd be lying—"

"Practice?" I couldn't resist adding,

"You're in rare company," she promised.

"Really?"

"The only one."

I found this dubious, but rather than question it, I turned my attentions on her, and then we made loveless love. When we had finished, her head lolled back and her eyes rolled with a narcotic gaze.

"You have such focus when you use your mouth, but then, when we're together, your attention span is so short. One minute you're looking at me, and the next you're staring at the wall."

"I'm in the void," I said, and hoped she could understand. It was not that I had a deficient span of attention but that I was being transported. I was voyaging through brand-new territories. The thoughts and images in my head came so fast and furious with her, I couldn't even communicate them. They flashed so rapidly that even the most frenetic and overedited piece of celluloid was a sluggish joke in comparison.

She climbed on top of me again, and it was as if a tornado of delight moved across my skin, touching down along the raw edges of my nerves, and broke up into sparkling showers of pleasure. But as it ended, as it always did, as it had to, I saw the dumpy motel I was in. Bright sunlight filtered through the cheap curtains and played out of key on my senses, illuminating the fact we were mostly strangers. I wished that it would rain one damn day out here, or be cloudy, or just turn to night already.

"What are you thinking?" she said quietly. It was a maddening, unanswerable question. I considered telling her the truth.

"If the Mets hadn't traded Mookie," I said instead, "they would have gone all the way that year." I turned my eyes to her face, to see whether insult or amusement had been provoked by my comment. But all I saw there was a vacant look of spent passion. It didn't matter what I said or did not say, or who I was or who she was. My head felt cotton-stuffed from all the absinthe I had guzzled, and I hurried into my clothes.

Taking her time, wrapped in a sheet, Ronnie kissed my back and asked, "We're still on for Saturday night, right?" I shrugged as I tied my left shoe.

I paid for the room before leaving, emptying my wallet. I was going to be thirty minutes late for my afternoon meeting with Jumper. I forced a pent-up burst of hysterical laughter out of myself. It hurt my throat, and I could swear I heard something crack in my chest. It felt like I had broken lightbulbs in there.

I hustled into Jackie's office, reporting snappily a half hour late for my rescheduled meeting with Jumper. Jackie greeted me with a roll of her eyes that let me know I had stepped in it again. I had the cool taste of licorice in my throat, and the dregs of a once buoyant good humor resting a bit lower.

"He's been looking for you," she said unnecessarily.

"Shall I go in?" I wondered.

"I just put him through to his mother in New York. She's ill. Let me buzz him," Jackie said, and worked the intercom.

"I'm holding for a nurse to put her on," Jumper said back through the speaker. "Send him in."

I walked into Sussman's office and found the producer behind his desk, toying with a firmly rolled Havana. He gave me an annoyed sidelong glance.

"I had car trouble on the way back from lunch," I offered, and seeing Sussman's pursed lips continued, "My engine temperature was running hot." I saw him still not believing me, so I added, "The needle shot all the way up,"

"All right," Sussman said, cutting me off, then into the phone said, "Thank you." He placed the receiver back in its cradle and put the call on speaker. A moment later, the far-off and sickly voice of a very old woman came into the room.

"Arnold?" she said, and cleared her throat.

"Yes, Mother, how are you feeling?" Sussman asked in a slightly modified version of his high-speed business timbre.

"Son. Are you coming?" she said in a heartrending tone.

"Yes, Mother. Are they taking good care of you?" Sussman inquired, the model son.

"When are you coming, son?" his mother asked, in a way that showed her faculties were not particularly sharp, and gave me the impression her time might not be long.

"Soon, Mom. I'm coming right away," Jumper said, almost faltering back to his usual brusque tone. "Let me speak to the nurse." There was a rustling on the other end of the phone, and Sussman clipped the end of his cigar, looking right at me.

"She's calling for you, sir," the nurse said. "She wants to know when you're coming to visit."

"Yes, I heard that. Make sure she has everything she needs and keep me posted on her condition." Sussman hung up and addressed me. "Lymphoma. Awful."

"When will you be going to New York?" I asked.

"I'm not," he said, devoid of feeling. "Too much happening around here." It sent a chill through me. There was no reason for me to have been privy to the call, and I realized it had been put on speaker phone as a show, for my edification. What's more, it had been a threat. If Sussman dealt with his ailing mother like that, there was little doubt of how he would handle me if the occasion arose.

"I see," I answered. Earnest work, or casual humor, might not be as appropriate a manner as a more warlike sense of self-preservation in my office dealings with this producer.

"We have this writer-director coming in. Patrick Hackman. We're going to discuss his project," Jumper went on, as if the conversation with his mother, possibly on her deathbed, hadn't even happened. I was distracted, mortified, and even saddened for the fading Ma Sussman. Yet I wondered how much pity she deserved, as she did have a hand in raising her son to be this way. Jackie buzzed Patrick Hackman's arrival, and he was shown in.

Stepping through the door, Hackman tossed his costly crocodile skin briefcase onto one of Jumper's unsightly chairs and walked right over to the dormant, computerized exercise cycle. Sussman met him there, with me close behind, and we all shook hands. Hackman was tall, wearing a buckskin jacket and ostrich cowboy boots, but his handshake was loose. He climbed on the cycle and simultaneously lit a cigarette. Jackie, still waiting in the doorway, asked if she could get him anything.

"Coffee," Hackman growled, "black." He had made a name for himself creating television series, a few that had been hits, some that hadn't. More important, they had simply been on the air. In television, like films, an unsuccessful credit was infinitely better than no credit at all. Hackman clearly fancied himself a man of action and, I was to learn, a man of letters as well.

"I was driving my race car last week," he started the meeting, "and got loose going into a curve at about a buck-o-five. Suddenly I was sure this was the story I was born to tell. . . ." Meanwhile, true to his description of the previous meeting, Jumper was enjoying the company of this man's man. Or acting that way.

"Pitch hasn't had a chance to read your script yet, Patrick," Sussman lied about my knowledge of the poorly written piece. Tripe was a word that came to mind often as I read it. Smiling broadly, Jumper continued. "We've been keeping it under wraps until the next draft. Would you like to run through it quickly so he'll know what we're talking about?" I knew this meant Sussman hadn't really read the script, and that he needed to hear the story before continuing. This was not a problem for the writer-director, who didn't mind the sound of his own voice.

"I'll take notes," I volunteered, grabbing a pad and pen.

Hackman talked about his movie, a kitschy coming-of-age

story, set against a rugged mountain backdrop, that contained a good deal of autobiographical elements. It was pure popcorn, and I was in the process of drawing a bucket of the fluffy stuff on my notepad when Hackman declared it a symbolic "Christ picture."

"The love story element of it is comparable to that of Adam and Eve." He used terms so loose, so grandiose, and full of so much momentum that I nearly forgot the two references were different tales from different Testaments altogether.

By the time he wound up, my latest afternoon of drink was wearing off, leaving me in a groggy state. I couldn't tell whether the main character died for someone else's sins or was tempted into sin by someone else. My notes reflected my poor attention. It became irrelevant, though, as Hackman went on about his picture. "I know what this movie is and no one else does, which is just the way I want it," he said proudly, as if this plan would yield a good piece of work in the collaborative medium of film.

"In terms of directors . . . ?" I asked carelessly, forgetfully, causing a pinched, uncomfortable look to appear on Jumper's face. Hackman sat up stick straight.

"I'm directing, of course," he said quickly.

"Of course," I agreed.

"If we can sell the idea to the studio, yes, naturally," Jumper said.

"They have two movies coming out this weekend. If they're hits, we just tell Kirkland it was his idea that I direct. He'll love it," Hackman said. It appeared holding the answer to everything fell within his gifts. The ridiculous thing was, it would probably work. If the pictures opened big, Kirkland, who had been in and out of grace with Lubin, would again be untouchable. The advance word wasn't good, however, so I wondered how it would work if the pictures bombed. A bruised studio head wouldn't be too keen on an untried director. If confidence was money, though, this Hackman had a million bucks.

"I'm like best friends with Alan Asher. He's committed. And that actress, the one who got the Oscar last year, what's that broad's name? . . . She's coming in her pants to work with me." Referring to his direction of these actors, Hackman even said, "I'll just have them read it exactly as it is on the page and not bump into the furniture."

Feeling deep in my marrow that it was unwise to do so, but needing to see what was on the other side of this supreme confidence, I uttered, "What if the films don't open well and Kirkland wants to play it safe with another director?"

Sussman, across the desk, looked beside himself.

Hackman, though, suffering no such pangs, stepped in and said, "Then Jumper will sell them on the idea. That's why he's the man."

"We'll all be interested in seeing how the pictures do, now . . ." Jumper said, smiling, unable to hide his pleasure at the strutting writer-director's conferment. He was interrupted by his phone buzzing. Picking it up, he said, "Okay, put her through," and then looked up and said, "My wife, it'll only take a second."

As we sat and waited, Hackman reached forward over the Exercycle's handlebars and plucked a script at random off a pile on Jumper's desk. He opened it, read a line, looked at me, and said, "Look at these stacks of shit. Look at this prose garbage . . . Just say what you mean already." I could see by the title that the screenplay was one of the few quality pieces in the system, but here was Hackman, blissfully unaware of the distinction.

"No getting around that prose in a piece of writing," I said, and wondered when the hell it was, what age I had been, when I had seen mystery and wonder in movies. When had they still provided secret worlds for me to vanish into, lasting escape and elation long after the images had disappeared from the screen? Now they were, for the most part, cookie-cutter stampings that mocked the viewer. They were laughing images that howled their derision at me, the lone watcher, enshrouded in darkness, being pulled along by the flickering light.

"God, there are bad writers out here," the great Hackman went on.

"You're one of them," my insides screamed. "Yours is the biggest piece of shit in the stack."

"This picture we're doing, I can write and direct the piss out of it," Hackman stated, sliding off the cycle and lighting another cigarette off the dying butt of his last. I was disgusted by the man, but couldn't deny a sneaking admiration for him, and those like him who populated the business. They just went ahead and got on with it regardless of how badly they did what they did. The meeting mercifully ended, as even the most numbing ones were wont to do, with Sussman making me sharply aware that I still had that screenplay to read for his lovely wife. I took the script and went home early.

. . .

Thankfully it was the weekend, for I was bone weary. Although there was never a respite from the reading, the script notes, the information trading, at least I would have a two-day hiatus from physically being in the office. I no longer knew what regular people did with their weekends. Whether they hiked or biked, spent time with wives or husbands, did origami, or sang opera. My life had narrowed here to this business alone. Once home, I sat down to read the script passed to me by Mrs. Sussman. After three pages I suspected the writer unskilled, and twenty pages in, it was confirmed. The writing was slack and blunt, and the script without hope. At least he was doing it, though, I thought of the writer, *and* he has a day job.

Had it been a regular screenplay I would have already hurled the thing toward a recycling bin, but this was Mrs. Sussman's pet project and I knew I had to force myself all the way through it. It was this way throughout the business—a worthy script that was not spoken for by someone of consequence could easily slip through the cracks, while a terrible mess like this one, merely vouched for by an influential player, got undeserved consideration. Rejecting this kind of project could even be considered politically dangerous depending on the relationships involved.

That night, upon finally finishing the grueling script, I wrote up coverage that spoke my true feelings on it—a vicious pass. I held back nothing, purging all my venomous feelings on this one project. It was a real bloodletting. The next morning, though, bright and early on my Saturday, I wrote up another set of coverage from the exact opposite point of view. Every line of praise I wrote, in the vague, semi-academic verbiage that the industry chose for its development-note vernacular, plucked at my sense of well-being and self-respect until I rang like a vibrating chord. I concentrated on making my comments believable yet glowing, typing as quickly as possible in order to distract myself from the welling up of sadness inside me. I poured myself a string of comforting opaline absinthes and promised myself I would never bastardize my work like this again.

Watching the sun go down like a surrendering flare, I realized with a sigh that I had spent all day on this wrenching project, and that I had promised this night to Ronnie Sylvan. I shot a glance at my answering machine's blinking light. It flickered in a coded progression. Checking the messages, I found several from her attempting to confirm our plans. I thought it odd that I hadn't once heard the phone ring. I was suddenly filled with trepidation at the prospect of seeing her that night, and even more frightened at the fact that I'd missed her calls. Sitting in the settling darkness, I tried to chart the progression of our relationship, but it eluded me. I could not determine whether the seeming shallowness of it masked a deep connection or if the opposite was true.

It had grown late, and I was not able to reach her when I called her back at home. I made a few more calls and found an acquaintance from the agency mailroom working late even though it was Saturday. I got him to give up Ronnie's home address from an agent's Rolodex. Driving to her house, I didn't concern myself with surprising her or upsetting her. Spontaneity had been established by her, so reciprocating should be no problem. Sure. I drove up her street in the hills and looked at the houses. Modern-style mansions lined the way, many with red Spanish tile roofs, all happy in their size and grandeur. When I had arrived in town not long ago, one of these large homes was to have been mine, where *I* would live within a few years, the only question being in which style—hacienda, renovated Victorian, California villa. But now I felt I'd never be able to climb the ladder and acquire one of these places. I was no longer sure I still wanted to.

I drove up to Ronnie's house. Pink, stately, and quiet, it rose above a high wooden fence and a closed gate with a buzzer. Her car and another, a Swedish sedan, were parked in front and I pulled in behind them. Upon checking, I found that the gate wasn't fully clicked shut. I pushed it open and walked through, continuing up to the door. I knocked several times despite the sudden feeling I didn't belong. Moments later she opened up, though, and again I was taken by her curvaceous form and her silky hair. The off-putting look on her face made me feel needy and foolish, but didn't remove the need, so when she moved aside, I stepped in.

I leaned over to give her a kiss that she withstood. "I hope I haven't created a monster," she said. "Have you been drinking that stuff all day?"

It was true. I had been more than nipping at my absinthe cache steadily throughout the afternoon, and I had continued through the evening, as I had been doing nearly every afternoon and evening since I had first tried it. Over the past weeks the collars of my shirts had begun to gap against my neck while my skin had taken on an ashen color. "Promise me you'll cut back on it," she commanded. Her concern sounded more motivated by her own possible culpability in having gotten me started than any tender caring, but I promised. She led me across a terra-cotta floor through darkened rooms furnished with large white chaise longues and wrought iron and glass tables. Modern halogen lamps pointed in acute angles toward various pieces of art, waiting to be illuminated. As well decorated as the house was, I was moved by how little evidence there was of anybody actually living in it. There were no magazines around, no books half read, used cups or plates, photographs, ashtrays. It was like a model unit in a housing development for all the personal touches it lacked. Perhaps it was this very quality that made it seem most like a perfect home for her.

"We've missed what I had planned," she said, and touched the back of her hand against her forehead as if she had a headache. She began walking away from me at a pace that discouraged me from tagging along. She had gone back into the house, toward the bedroom, I supposed, when the buzzer sounded. I heard her voice from the recesses of the house. "That's my dinner, will you pay him please? There's money in the bowl on the hallway table."

"Tip?" I called out, finding the tortoiseshell bowl.

"Whatever." I lifted the bowl's lid and saw hundreds and fifties piled on top of and curling and snaking around each other. I stared at the bills for a moment, then began stuffing them into the pockets of my pants and didn't stop until I reached the bottom of the bowl. I replaced the lid and went to the door, where I paid a Korean driver delivering Moroccan food. I had a wad of bills in change remaining as I carried the sacks in, and passing the bowl in the hall, I considered putting the change in it. Instead I stuck this money in my pocket too. I could recall nothing in my life that resembled this act, but now it seemed part of a natural progression.

I crossed into the kitchen and thought about setting out the meal for her, but dumped the bag on the table and went looking for a glass and any absinthe she might have. I rifled her cabinets and at last found a small bottle and the other things I needed. I threw together a quick drink, downed it, and poured another as she entered. She hadn't changed clothes, but whatever she had done while away had renewed her energies. Fresh-faced and a little flushed, she noted my drink without expression and began to lay out the food expertly.

"I always order a lot," she said by way of explaining as she set the table elegantly for two. I watched, leaning back in my chair, sipping my drink insolently. I hadn't come here for dinner, but if she wanted to cater to me, then so be it. She ate off shiny plates, and stabbed the spicy food with glittering tableware. Sitting at her table, I faced the question of what I should do next. So far she'd been leading me around like a pup on a check cord, but that had been fine with me. When I looked for clues as to why I was so drawn to her and my life here, the only time I could contemplate the riddle effectively was while I was coming. It was then I seemed to be breathing in a rarefied air of knowledge emanating from her. In those scarce and precious moments things became clear to me, and I understood the hunger and hollow of my heart. It was madness to pursue the taunting emptiness we created, but the loneliness of this crowded town had become intolerable. I was falling for her because I had to fall for something. A ridiculous reason. She had smashed the old logic, though, without providing new ideals, and now only the lack of ideals altogether seemed attractive. And I was powerless to extract myself from her taunting brashness, her short skirts, lace, and g-strings, her plunging décolletage.

I was in a kind of trance as we finished dinner. Had we had any conversation? I heard only my promises to myself that I wouldn't show up like this again. I told myself I'd better get ahold of myself, and try to figure out why I was so powerless and so attracted. My shoulders slumped in exhaustion, and my mind refused to think at all anymore. I just looked at her, and I looked down at the plates on the table, all in disarray. The now empty bottle was tipped over and a small green pool emanated from its mouth. When I reached out toward her, she didn't reach back eagerly, but she didn't resist either, and that was all I sought. I ran my hands and mouth over her as we sank to the floor. The tile was hard and cold, and her skin so soft it seemed handfuls of it dripped from my palms at every touch.

Moments later we were in her bed. The bedroom, just like the rooms at the hotels, and the rest of the house, was completely without sign of her presence. Maybe she didn't really live here either. We did our dance with each other. A dance that was rapidly becoming as necessary to me as air and water. Horrible cries of ecstasy rang in my ears. I kissed her to stop them, and through the panting I looked down at her and blurted, "I love you . . ." It must have been the absinthe that had ahold of me, the burrowing, prying fingers of the wormwood tearing the lid off my control.

I looked down into her face and saw it so unchanged that I was confused for a moment. I went to say something else, felt my mouth move, but heard no sound issue forth. It was then I realized with relief that nothing, no words, had actually passed my lips. I fell off into a fitful blackness during which I dreamed of a familiar brown, furrowed piece of land, and a little farmhouse with a light hanging above the porch. I did not know where it was, but someone I knew lived there. I dreamily could not place who, but it might have been me. . . .

I awoke with a start. It could have only been a little while later, and although the room was dark and I couldn't see her, I felt the distant pose she lay in. Then I focused in on her eyes, which were open, looking at me.

"What?" I said.

"You," she said back.

"I said something," I half asked.

"It doesn't matter."

"Yes, it does," I said, feeling doomed.

"You call out when you come," she let me know. "Strange things I don't understand. A certain word—"

I cut her off. "It's a bad habit."

"It's always disappointing to learn someone's bad habit," she breathed.

"Have I done it before?" I wondered.

"This is the first time it's mattered," she said, and right away I knew I should leave. I wished I could just be gone. I saw how much she preferred her clean and uncluttered home, her aseptic room. I dressed quickly, trying with my limited faculties to locate my clothes in the darkness. I was amazed at her poise, at my own blundering, at my vulnerability to the hateful drink that thickened and loosened my tongue. When I was dressed, I crossed over to her and silently reached out a hand to touch her on the shoulder. With a nearly inaudible rustle she moved out from under it, leaving me stroking the air.

I walked gingerly down the hall, as if my delicate silence could erase my presence, and beyond that my whole life. I closed the gate behind me quietly, as if it were the thing at which I was most professional. I got behind the wheel and began the drive home. As I drove, the less-ness particular to this town began to creep into my car and engulf me. I drove all the way back and had nearly reached my destination, finally turning down Poinsettia, when I looked up with fading eyes, and saw the famous sign that had magnetized millions. It was blurred in the distance on the mountainside, but I swore it read *WORMWOOD*.

CHAPTER NINE

An earthquake awakened me rudely Monday morning, slamming the blinds against my windows. The entire building that housed the cracker box rolled like it was on top of some giant humpbacked animal. Since I had come here, I'd seen I couldn't even count on the earth's standing still beneath me. Long past being frightened by the tremors of this kind that occasionally added to the hazards of life in town, though, I relished witnessing the power of something so completely outside human control, a force not under the influence of the business and its brokers. When the building stopped shaking I rose and checked my schedule. I had lunch with Jumper and the new vice president today, and had just enough time to squeeze in my appointment at the opthamologist's office.

On my way to the eye doctor, I brooded over the consequences of the weekend's events with Ronnie. I had tried to reach her on the phone several times on Sunday morning and afternoon, and by nighttime, when she still hadn't answered, I resorted to leaving messages on her hated machine. Three of them. Finally, late on Sunday night I had driven to her house, as I swore I would not, but found the gate locked and no answer when I buzzed the intercom. I had climbed the gate and pounded on the door for several minutes, but still no one answered. The house had been dark, but that was no guarantee she wasn't at home.

Sitting down in the doctor's waiting room, I tried to vanquish these thoughts from my mind, and picked up the latest issue of a glossy entertainment business rag that lay on the table in front of me. I was amazed and horrified to see that the cover featured "The Renaissance of Absinthe, Town's Latest Seduction." Every story, fad, trend, or bit of gossip that had been vilified or glorified either in print, on television, or on the screen had been robbed of cachet by the grotesque revelation. The attention that an interesting item would receive removed any subtle allure it might have previously held and left it standing naked and out in the open. It was a "warts and all" approach that people here had an insatiable appetite for, but to have one's affliction reported as trendy pop culture was the height of banality.

With hysterical fascination I ripped open the issue, found the article, and raced through it. The same magazine had, in a previous edition, swaggeringly revealed how stylish it had recently become again for models and actresses to work as high-priced call girls. It now took the same simple-minded and provocative approach to absinthe, my steadfast companion. Blah, blah, blah, banned in the early part of the century, blah, blah, blah, the supposed ruin of many painters and poets, blah, blah, blah, secret distilleries still bottling it and smuggling it in, blah, blah, blah, selective clubs making it available to the new café society, blah, blah, blah, once thought to cure many ills, also thought to cause seizures and insanity, blah, blah, blah . . . The article went on to make public the first and last haven from the common that I had found, to strip away any remaining mystery and magic that life here held for me.

Sweating and disheveled, I was at last shown into my appointment. Dr. Sobel was game-show-host handsome with a deep umber tan. His shirt and tie were of the starchy and florid variety that would play well on the lot. His collar fit perfectly. He had me sit and try an eye chart projected on the far wall of the exam room.

"Give me the first line," he said, and I did with no problem. However, as I reached the bottom rows, the letters were obscured and I began to guess.

"Do you read a lot?" Dr. Sobel wondered.

"An extreme amount."

"Poor-quality print?"

"Screenplays. Many generations photocopied," I answered.

"Give me row eight," he said.

"L, X . . . W," I tried.

"No, no, that's an H . . ." he murmured and swung a heavy piece of machinery in front of my face. He dialed through several lenses in front of each of my eyes until we had achieved maximum clarity.

"If it's in any way possible, I'd like you to cut down on the reading," he counseled, pulling away the machine and beginning to write out my prescription.

"Not much chance of that," I said.

"Well, take this. My frame department can outfit you right away." He reviewed my chart. "I see here you work at Iceberg Productions. . . . My son wrote a screenplay, high school antics in Beverly Hills, how about if I send it over and you give it a read?" He plied me with a tawdry smile. I noticed that the cream that lent him his deep umber shade was rubbing off on his shirt collar.

"Sure." I nodded and walked out toward the frame department.

A short time later, I emerged from the office with a new pair of corrective glasses. I drove slowly up to the studio, through the splintering sunlight, underneath the shadowless palm trees, and looked at the road with punishingly clear vision. I walked into Jackie's office. "It'll be in the executive dining room," she told me, "and I sure hope you wrote up Mrs. Sussman's project."

I mumbled in the affirmative and, briefcase in hand, marched across the lot. Along the way I couldn't help but notice the hushed tone of the place. There was the scent of blood in the air, and a feeling of violence about the lot. Realizing what day it was, I quickly went to Chip's office.

"How'd the pictures open this weekend?" I asked him.

"*The Man in Charge* was a total dud. It made about two million five. *Cub Reporters* was even worse," Chip gushed in a strange singsong way.

"What'd the per-screen averages look like?" I asked.

"Less than a thousand," he answered almost joyfully.

The numbers spelled complete disaster. Per-screen averages that low would have been grounds for corporal punishment had the law allowed it.

I too felt a momentary malevolent burst of humor in my chest at the wonderful failure of others. "Any aftermath?"

"Tears are flowing," Chip said, with the same gleam in his eye that he had displayed in the projection booth. I checked my watch and hurried on.

The executive dining room was the typical pastiche of my life in town. Bell and Atkinson were feeding at tables on opposite ends of the room. Kessler was lunching with Lubin. Even that bastard Feller was sitting with his back to the wall, doing a little tap dance for Halifax. I saw Jumper and a sharp-featured, somewhat attractive woman embroiled in a contest of mutual admiration over a pair of passion fruit iced teas, and headed over to them. The only one missing on the scene was Kirkland.

"Hello, Jumper, and . . ." I said, extending my hand.

"Kathleen. Kathleen Sanger," the woman said, standing up and giving me a handshake that Patrick Hackman could have taken a lesson from. Still seated, Sussman regarded me with irritation.

"Sorry I'm late," I said, wondering if I would ever get anywhere on time again. A waiter showed up and started distributing dishes.

"I took the liberty of ordering for you," Sussman said, punishing my lack of punctuality. "Nice spectacles."

"Thank you," I said, ignoring his intended snub and cutting into a veal parmigiana so heavy and rich that no sane person would order it for lunch.

"You have that script written up for my wife?" Jumper said as he and Kathleen began on their crisp Waldorf salads. "She'll be joining us at the end of the meal to go over it."

"Sure do," I answered, stretching a string of cheese to arm's length on my fork, and wondering which way I was going to play it when it came time to hand over my coverage.

"I was just telling Jumper about this absolutely fabulous article I read on absinthe," Kathleen said, clueing me in to their conversation. "We were discussing whether or not there was a movie in the 'new absinthe café scene.' " I was filled with instant irrational hatred for her.

"What do you think, Nathan?" Jumper asked, as if he wanted the wrong answer so he could cuff me into line.

"Van Gogh said his paintings of cafés tried to express the idea that they were places where a man could ruin himself, go mad, or commit a crime," I said, in an attempt to be oblique.

"That's a yes," Kathleen and Jumper excitedly agreed.

"I'm envisioning a marketing report breaking down cities by the amount of cafés and coffee houses that they contain," Sanger said.

"If we could tap that audience, then the idea has potential." Jumper nodded over his Waldorf, which looked quite light and fresh compared to my meal.

They then went on to discuss the slate of projects that were in development, while I had to force myself to stay involved.

I saw right away that this Kathleen Sanger, a woman I recognized by both name and carriage as Ronnie Sylvan's friend,
was a brass tack, a piece of agate. It was her first day and
she was trying to create a good impression, but as she spoke
on and on, I found her so aggravating that I noticed my feet
drumming a spastic tattoo—completely beyond my control—
against the floor. As I stared at her calculating eyes and the
dried flecks of pancake makeup that tried in vain to cover
strange, dark blemishes on her face, I found my hands balling
up into fists beneath the table. As she went from "irreverant"
to "cute and charming" for Sussman's enjoyment, it was as
grating to me as gears changing without a clutch.

At last the waiter came and cleared the plates, and it
seemed that the meal was drawing to a close. Around the
dining room other tables began to finish as well. Lubin and
Kessler came by to pay their respects to Sussman, shaking his
hand and winking at him in some silent conferment of their
regard. Bell and Atkinson did the same, and while a healthy
round of ass-kissing was Sussman's due on any day, this display seemed a little extreme.

"Well, well, aren't you popular," Kathleen trilled.

"What's up, Jumper?" I asked bluntly.

No longer surprised by my straightforwardness, Jumper
leaned in conspiratorily and said, "The studio took quite a
bath this weekend with their two pictures. It won't be official
for a few days, but Kirkland went out with the bathwater."

"You're the new chief?" Kathleen asked. I already knew
the answer. Jumper bowed his head in benediction. Eighteen
months, and if the first set of pictures under one's tenure

weren't hits, then one was out, and while Kirkland was no exception, Jumper wouldn't be either in a year and a half.

"Well, that was a short run for me," Kathleen said with complete calm.

"Oh, you'll be coming over to the main house with me," Jumper let her know in a way that would have made me feel safer had he said "with us." But before another moment went by, a woman walked in, distracting our line of conversation and drawing the attention of the whole room to her. She preened in the notice, as if every room she had ever entered had reacted similarly. The reason for this was not due to her physical appearance, though, for she was devoid of aesthetic beauty. Rather, every move the lady made seemed to create a racket. She was short, precariously close to dumpy, but not there yet, with a bonnet of knotty hair that had been whipped and coerced into a semblance of a silky sheen. Her outfit took pains to be elegantly casual, but too many accessories, regimental in their uniformity, betrayed her intention, and gave the impression that from head to toe she was simply overwrought. Jumper sagged a little upon her entrance. There was no mistaking that this was his wife, and that every time he saw her and realized anew that she was, a bit of disappointment and dismay was visited upon him. He gathered himself immediately, in a way that despite everything made me feel for him, and rose to kiss her hello. She blocked the attempt, however, uttering loudly, "Oh, don't touch me, its sooo beastly hot out there I'm going to melt."

Kathleen jumped up, introduced herself and commented on her own attire, a dress shirt and blue blazer. "I know, I know. I wore *this* because this morning it looked cloudy and gloomy, and I thought it would be cool. Also because I'm a lesbian," she added in a frank way that made them all laugh, and caused me to admire her a little too through my previous loathing. The remark seemed to create an immediate bond between her and Jumper's wife, introduced to me as Naomi. I remembered some gossip furtively whispered to me by Kai, in almost unrecognizable English, about Mrs. Sussman having been a little-known, but enthusiastic, lesbian herself. Kai had related similar rumors about Jumper regarding his homosexuality too. At the time I'd had little reason to pay attention, other than to appreciate the symmetry in the tales, and yet there was no denying that Kathleen and Naomi were getting on quite nicely.

"Kathleen is going to sit in with us," Jumper said to his wife. "She's read the script also."

"What did you think of it, dear?" Mrs. Sussman asked her.

"I thought it was wonderful," she beamed, lighting up Mrs. Sussman. "Of course, it needs *some* work."

"Naturally," Mrs. Sussman agreed. "What did you think, Nathan?" she asked, surprising me a little by her recognition of my existence, which implicitly carried a low-voltage threat.

I drew a deep breath and considered the fight that would ensue should I venture my real opinion. A kind of exhaustion overcame me at the prospect, and suddenly there was the easy and amicable road in front of me. "I agree," I chimed in, hating myself. Then, as if to prove a point to my own integrity, I went on to enthusiastically espouse all the script's smaller details, just as I had in my second set of notes, which I quickly produced from my briefcase. The meeting carried on in a rosy fashion from there, Jumper quietly watching the proceedings with a sagacious smile.

My reward was swift. "Nathan's going to be the studio's story editor as of next week, dear," Jumper said. "He'll run the entire Story Department."

"Isn't that nice?" she murmured.

"Isn't it?" I chorused along with her.

Official word came out in the trades, and I was forced to deal with many of the details of a new regime taking over the studio. Throughout the rest of the week I, along with Jackie, acted as a tactical sergeant, coordinating the logistics of the move from the offices in the Producers Building to Jumper's new headquarters in The Bunker. The Bunker. The building managed both a martial and labyrinthine quality at the same time. Each floor and office was laid out in a neo-corporate blandness. The structure's modern design, with halfhearted nods to several traditional styles of architecture, resulted in a network of corridors as deceptive in their uniformity as they were uniform in their deception. Newcomers to the lot were constantly lost and late for meetings, wandering down mirror-image hallways, breathing in the fumes of flat gray paint that were still strong in the air despite the building's completion a few years earlier.

Down in the basement, in antiseptic quarters that thumped with the sound of high-powered air conditioning, I took over the Story Department. While upstairs, behind massive, sunlight-admitting plate-glass windows, Jumper's art collection and exercise bicycle were moved in, I worked to organize the subterranean space full of scripts, each hard-copy draft coded with different-color pages, and coverage on microfiche and computer disks, into a massive library housing most of the projects from around town as well as the studio's own pictures. Had the changeover occurred six, or even three, months earlier, I would have been able to attack my new position with unmatched enthusiasm. As it was, however, reading scripts had now become a chore. When I slipped on my new glasses to begin, it felt like strong magnets pulling at my eyes, stretching them outward from my skull.

There was also the nuisance of Kathleen Sanger for me to contend with. She was everywhere now, in all development meetings, calling around to all the agencies for the new material, nipping along at Jumper's heels. She brought in a massive volume of fresh projects, all of it flowing into my department for my readers and me. I had four professional readers under me, who were paid on a per-script basis and were even more weathered than myself. Not only was Kathleen a constant presence, but she and I rarely saw eye to eye on content, style, or much else. We had an uncomfortable way of dealing with each other too. Each of us was crystal clear in what we were saying, but somehow our words met with a kind of atmospheric interference that kept us from receiving each other's messages accurately.

Ronnie had become an apparition. I would call, both home and office, and leave word, but she would never return. On an inspiration born of a police procedural, I resorted to going to lunch and dinner in all the restaurants that we had been in together, or that I had heard her talk about. When that yielded no results, I continued on to the most expensive "in" spots I could think of, hoping for a chance meeting. Again I had no luck in finding her, and only succeeded in distressing my finances and encountering other people from the business I did not want seeing me alone. I could practically hear my stock in town dropping despite my new job title.

I was hardly ever home anymore either. My workload at the studio, and the sluggish pace at which I now addressed it, called for hours and hours of unpaid overtime every day. Since Jumper had taken over, the studio was running on a skeleton crew of executives and support staff until new positions could be created and some old ones could be filled again. The result was a serious time crunch on many projects. Instead of going home, I would often work until dinnertime, go out to one trendy restaurant or another in search of Ronnie, and come back to work again. I kept some clothes in a locker in the men's room, and the executive bathroom upstairs had a shower that I had access to. I would work late into the night, sometimes past four in the morning, the quality of my work declining all the while and all the while caring less. Nobody seemed to notice quality anyway, for just as with a lousy credit, poor work was vastly preferable to not having it done. I hardly even wondered anymore why I was working so hard, having somehow passed through from free will to a state of yoked drudgery. I never felt more pathetic than when I padded down the hall past conference rooms and offices heading for a five A.M. shower, wearing only a towel, and ran into some assistants leaving for the night. Instead of sharing a sense of camaraderie, I was greeted by their mockery.

At one point, despite our adversarial feelings, I broke down enough to talk to Kathleen Sanger about Ronnie. "Have you seen her lately?" I said in a tone I intended as casual but which came across as miserable.

"Yes," she answered, reeling me in.

"Did you know that we were friendly?" I asked her.

"She mentioned you did something for me when I was interviewing with Jumper." She spoke derisively, as if she knew the extent to which I had really helped her, and was giving me no credit where none was due.

"Send her my regards," I said feebly, feeling I had lost any leverage I might have had in my dealings with either one of them.

"You should just call her and say hello," Kathleen suggested. I saw she was aware of the state of things, and her comment had the effect of a kick to the abdomen.

After several weeks of this lifestyle, I was summoned to Jumper's home for a morning meeting, a review of the troops. Arriving promptly at nine o'clock, I was discouraged to see Sanger's car, a gleaming black Volvo, already parked in front of the mansion's coach house. Jackie's car was there as well. As Kai opened the door for me and gave me a conspiratorial nod, I found myself returning it now, feeling more serf-like kinship with this man than I ever would with my fellow executives. Kai showed me past the pantry, where Mrs. Sussman was in the middle of one of her famous tirades. Jackie was the recipient this time. ". . . your job is to make him comfortable, and to figure out what that means . . ." Her voice buzzed with a beady edginess over Jackie's gritted silence. As I walked by, I heard Jackie sniff back a tear.

It took a virtual public relations machine to keep the flattering stories about Naomi Sussman coming, like the one about her being down to earth and driving a Jeep. On more than one occasion I had seen flacks leaving the lot who worked for the p.r. firm Jumper retained to reverse public perception of his wife's monstrousness. I certainly hadn't been fooled by my first encounter with her. I knew her saccharine attitude was as thin as a layer of paint: one scratch and pure malice would show through. Kai continued on, leading me to the living room, where I was told to sit and wait.

Finally inside the once impenetrable house, I took in the decor and was struck by the dusty, ancient feel of the place. While Jumper's offices reflected his wife's taste—all new and thrown together, expensive but ugly—the house was closer to his—worn, and all glory past. The carpets were thin, and the furniture cushions seemed to contain foul odors of unhealthy days gone by. I knew how expensive everything was, that was a given, but there was nothing about the rooms that caused me to envy the Sussmans for living there. I was aware that they had a screening room downstairs, where they would get together with other studio heads and assorted bigwigs for famed weekly showings of each other's recent releases. What had become of my ancient burning desire to be amongst that cadre? The flame had burned lower and lower, and was now nearly extinguished.

Moments after I was seated, Kathleen Sanger appeared in the doorway. She signaled me to follow her down the hall. "I was in with Jumper, but he got a call from Senator Hanson," she said as if privy to secret knowledge. Hanson was presidential timber, and a supposed friend to the industry. Sanger escorted me into Jumper's office, where he was still on the phone. I listened to Jumper, who was oddly shiny-eyed, talk from behind his desk. The topic was the many ills from which the country suffered. As he spoke I looked closely at him and decided he was on some kind of pharmaceutical ride. There was a vacancy behind his pinpoint pupils that seemed windows to what was inside him—even more vacancy.

"Yes, Senator, the bay," he lilted. "Got to clean up that bay . . . and the hole in the ozone. That damned ozone . . . nothing more important than women's rights . . . just what I was going to say *except* minority rights . . . but nothing does move voters like the unemployment issue . . . oh, you bet a reduced cap gains tax would be popular around here . . ." To the uninformed the call scaled the heights of civic-minded concern. But I knew that for Hanson the call was about scrounging campaign funds, and for Sussman it was power brokering.

"Yes, Senator, twenty-five thousand per table . . . Of course I'll sit at yours," Jumper said. I could see his pursed lips and his earnest concern about the issues, and I could picture Hanson's on the other end of the line. Jumper's blissful, glazed expression belied what he was really thinking, though—"How special you make me feel, knowing someone in your position. And what can you do for me? What can I gain?" For Kathleen, looking on in rapt fascination, the call must have been further proof that she was on the fast track.

"I may be the man, but you're going to be the next president of these United States," Jumper concluded and hung up the phone with a sated smile.

I never thought I would be glad to see Atkinson and Chick Bell enter a room, but a moment later when they arrived, ushered in by Mrs. Sussman, I was. Upon her arrival, I noted that Naomi Sussman's state was completely fugue-like, unlike the one I had seen her in moments earlier. Now she was much subdued. There was a bit of slackness in her jaw where it had just been overwrought, and she had a faraway expression on her face, as if she were trying to remember something that wasn't very important anyway. I recognized her aspect as a prescription drug-induced stupor similar to Jumper's. Bell and Atkinson seemed oblivious to the fact that she was smiling like a zombie as they munched away on scones and croissants, but Kathleen cocked an eyebrow at her. I saw the wheels turning in her head as to how she could work this for an advantage. Not figuring out how to do so immediately, she simply filed the information away and turned on a big smile.

Before long Jumper clipped a cigar, lit up, and took the room with his usual cloud of authority and smoke, which pumped up the energy and uneasiness of all in attendance. The subject of the meeting, which now came to order, was casting possibilities for Hackman's film. The writer-director's project had miraculously survived the change in command, a time when many projects were slashed and dumped. This gathering was a secret prelude to the casting meeting that would take place with Hackman later on, once the studio had aligned its own priorities. Hackman, for all his bravado and limitations, was still the project's creative force, and this meeting, this conspiracy of ours, was just another attempt to subjugate his creativity to our own ends.

Everyone pored over their casting lists. I pored over a blank legal pad, jotting down someone else's good idea once in a while, and occasionally volunteering a random name from one of my past favorite films. I was now naturally carrying on in the Wormwood fashion, unprepared and making suggestions with no thought of feasibility. If I could continue in this manner, I would be a vice president within two years. In the next few years after that I could run a production company. Distracted as such, I went a bit far. I put forth the name of Kessler's famous deceased client. "How about Hume Sanders?"

"He's dead, you know," Kathleen Sanger rebuffed me.

"Of course," I returned smoothly. "I meant someone like him. A Hume Sanders type. Someone *Hume Sander-esque.*" The logic seemed to appeal to Bell, but annoyed Sussman.

"Enough with the screwing around, Pitch," he slurred a bit sloppily in his intoxication.

Before the meeting could go on, Kai came tearing excitedly into the room. "Big accident happen outside," he said over and over, "Oh, big smash accident."

Like an awkwardly moving caravan headed up by two stoned Pied Pipers, we serpentined out with the Asian houseman. What we found just down the street was a destroyed economy car. It was Atkinson's. Unlike Bell, who drove a sporty convertible that was washed biweekly on the lot, Atkinson was not a favorite son, and drove a holdover from his college days. Since he had arrived last that morning, he had been unable to park in the crowded driveway, and had left it cresting the steep hill Sussman's house rested upon. The car's parking brake had quit, and it had careened down the hill, hurtled through a neighbor's azaleas, and gone to smash against a tree.

There was copious dismay, and speculation as to possible liability, and as the group surveyed the wreck and sorted matters out, Kai remarked quietly to me, "That was his car? He must not be a very high executive."

Later in the day I recalled the comment when, as part of supposed studio restructuring, Atkinson got pink-slipped. It could have been due to a number of reasons, but the houseman's analysis belied something true behind the misfortune. In a town full of prowling dogs looking to mount a weaker one, the accident hinted at a void in the defenses, a loser's luck, and Atkinson had been instantly, ruthlessly weeded out. That afternoon, although I felt little remorse at seeing him go, I thought it high time I address certain matters such as these. On studio letterhead, I wrote a terse memorandum.

Memorandum

To: Creative Group
From: The Top
Re: Comportment

Please be advised that:
1. *Shabby clothes*
2. *Rundown cars*
3. *Physical shortcomings*
4. *Personal problems*

*will not be tolerated in the workplace. You are hereby cau-
tioned that any of the above will heretofore be considered
reason for temination.*

With glee and disregard for consequence I copied a stack
of them and sent the memo into general circulation via inter-
office mail. It hit the lot with a splat and began to spread
throughout town at a pace that left Sussman, Sanger, and the
rest of the brass worrying about potential fallout in morale. A
copy even reached me by fax, sent from my counterpart at
another studio who must not have realized that I would have
received it interoffice already had I not been behind it in the
first place. By day's end Kathleen Sanger, at her request, had
been made Gestapo in charge of finding out who was culpable.

Later in the week, while sitting in my office awaiting my
own termination, or word of further upheaval resulting from
my memo, I instead got word that a cast had been locked in
on Hackman's film. The casting had come out just the way
the studio wanted it, just the way it had been planned at the
morning meeting at Jumper's house. Only Hackman thought
that he had decided. The lead was not Alan Asher, but another
major star who would receive twelve million for the role and
had already submitted a preferred crew list of thirty relatives,
friends, and sycophants to be hired on at the studio's expense.
The star was several years older than the part described, and
choosing a younger actor would have shown more integrity,
but Hackman was now fully behind the choice. While Hackman had originally wanted no-names in supporting roles,

Jumper had finally swayed him with a "Come on, Patrick, we're in the big leagues now, swing for the fences." He had agreed, and Jumper was once again worthy of his reputation as "the man."

As for me, I had gotten all this information secondhand, since I had been eased out of the meeting process. The supposed reason given was a new separation between Story Department and Creative Group. The real reason was that Kathleen had convinced Jumper I was not of benefit. They were right to cut me out too. I was an attitude problem, and every time I showed how little I cared, I drew them closer to witnessing the hollowness of the whole process. I waited for the merciful onset of night and recognized that this completion of principal casting marked the first tangible step that had been taken past development on any project I had been involved with. I had no feeling of triumph or hope at this. Nor did I feel cynicism or despair. I did receive an invitation to go along with Hackman, the Creative Group, and some of the cast to celebrate the picture's upcoming green light that night, but all I felt was emptiness.

Although I knew it was unwise, before I could go, I had to be enveloped in a haze of absinthe. Since that last night with Ronnie, due in part to her comments, and in part because of my work and the expense, but largely because of the lousy magazine exposé that Kathleen had found so goddamned riveting, I hadn't wanted to drink any more of it. It had lost its first-blush allure. Unfortunately, saying good-bye to it just wasn't that easy. I had managed to cut my morning rations a bit, but by afternoon the familiar bottle in my desk drawer began softly calling. By nightfall, with desk lights popping on all around, it became too difficult to resist, and I would begin.

Tonight, setting up my first glass, before I could indulge, there was a timid knock on my door, and the small, bald, still deeply sun-darkened head of Jared from the agency mailroom peeked in.

"Jared, how are you?" I said, surprised to see him.

"Nathan," my ex-tormentor returned.

"How's the agency?" I asked, aware that it had recently merged with another to become even more powerful, but a new overage of heavy egos at play were making it an even worse working environment than it had been before.

"I'm not there anymore. They automated the mail-routing system and hired a twenty-one-year-old computer programmer to supervise it," he said distantly.

I imagined the depths to which this must have humbled the man and stripped him of his identity. "What can I do for you?"

"I'm looking for work."

"I'm not sure how the mail run is supervised here, but—" I began.

"I was hoping to get into development. Perhaps start with some script reading," he said with an effort.

"Have you ever done this kind of work before?" I asked.

"You know I know all about scripts, Nathan."

"Do I?" I thought to myself. Had I foreseen this moment back when I was under the crushing weight of this man's thumb, I would have roared with laughter and vengeance and meted out proper retribution. Now, however, I felt only dismay.

This signaled a change in the order of things as I had come to know them, and I was not at all comfortable with the new hierarchy.

"How are your wife and kids?" I asked quietly.

"My wife divorced me. She thinks I'm gay," Jared said with a starkness that could only have been born from copious suffering.

"Are you?"

"I don't think I care anymore. The kids stayed with me."

"We pay a hundred dollars for screenplays. Hundred fifty for overnight rush. Books and longer projects up to two hundred." I handed him a script and some sample coverage.

"You know, Nathan, we've started a support group, a bunch of ex-employees of the agency. . . . We discovered that working there did something to us, broke us. . . . Would you like to come to a meeting?"

"Leave the information on my voice-mail," I said, noncommittal. He nodded and left. I finally had an enemy behind the eight ball, and I had let him go. Not only that, I had given the man a job. I pictured Kessler, Shelby, Ronnie, Kathleen, Jumper, even Bell if he could have figured out how, each knocking the man's head off had they been in my situation. I think I just wanted to get him out of the way quickly and get on with my absinthe. I drank my potent liquor, snapped off the light, and went to join the crowd.

Dinner was had in a restaurant high on a hill overlooking the breathtaking array of lights that was the city at night. The place, decorated like a Berber tent, was a chic den of exclusivity that fairly disallowed anybody from outside the business. It was the first of five eateries owned by a man who was saluted throughout town for his culinary skills. Hardly a thing on the menu was prepared without cilantro or shiitake mushrooms. The rest of the dishes contained either sun-dried tomatoes, chili peppers, or radicchio, were bathed in a revolting pesto sauce, served seared on a hot rock, coated in mango chutney, or made with several other abstract ingredients that only served to make a regular dish disagreeable. Despite it being such a trendy spot, I once again failed to sight Ronnie Sylvan.

Flanking Jumper were Kathleen on one side and an oddly familiar-looking, extremely old Asian man. I searched the man's craggy face and inscrutable eyes for a hint of recognition, but found none. He ate only steamed vegetables from a tiny bowl, and had been introduced as Jumper's personal herbalist and healer. Having one's medicine man along at all times was the latest indulgence for the very wealthy. Next to me was Bell, beside him Hackman the director. Beside him sat a young comic actor named Billy Adragna, who was on the rise due to his passionate and fiery performances and despite his not being very good-looking. He had been cast in a supporting role in the film. Several other people—from marketing, publicity, physical production—also circled the table. Red wine and chatter flowed as I looked on and tried to keep down my lacquered tuna with papaya mint salad and *wakami*.

"I'm going to find out who's behind the memo," Sanger assured Jumper. "I've already got some clues."

"This business ages you in dog years, just like working in

the White House," the head of marketing said to Adragna, the comic actor sitting next to her.

"Two shot, I walk into the room." Hackman graced me with an anecdote in directorial terms. "Smash cut to this stripper from the club that night who wanted a part in the movie— she's waiting in my bed . . . Dissolve to morning and she's still there . . ." I stood and excused myself.

Returning from a men's room dram of absinthe, I was in time to see the Asian man stand behind Jumper, place an acupunctural needle in his skull, and give an adjustment to a pressure point in the producer's neck.

"Aaahhh . . ." Jumper's scream of agony rang out, bringing the entire restaurant to a halt. In a voice nearly as loud he then added, "I feel great!" He twisted his head about, apparently more freely than he'd been able to before. "It helps the digestion too," Jumper added for the benefit of all. The shaman made a small bow and retook his seat.

As the restaurant crowd thinned out and several of the more conservative, sensitive, or less upwardly mobile members of our entourage departed, the remainder of the group went on by limousine to Mons Veneris, a place where for hard cash one could wrestle supple women in mud or oil. The group walked into a cavernous building that thundered with the sound of rock music and sirens, and we were blitzed by epileptic lights and dry-ice smoke. We saw men applying oil with neurosurgeons' precision to waves of undulating, bitter-beautiful reptiles who continuously emerged from the back in different fantasy-stripping costumes, from police officer to soldier, to cheerleader, to construction worker, to Little Bo Peep. It was a frightening display of diverting sexual lies, told so boldly no one dared dispute them. Everything occurred in perfect safety with no chance of disease too, since the wrestlers got the night off whenever their herpetic sores were open, the management wanted us all to know.

Our troop, which included Hackman, Billy Adragna, the head of physical production, Chick Bell, Kathleen Sanger, Sussman's healer, and several others took over the front ringside row of the place. Then, in the dark, smoky serraglio atmosphere, we began to be slathered by $5,000 cancerous cannonball breasts. The performers kissed and gyrated on one and all, to the group's delight, for the most meager of tips stuffed inside their g-strings. Jumper Sussman, in his new found Zen-like healed state, was funding the entire outing on the studio's expense account and presided over our row.

The men in the place, other than our group, were foreign businessmen knowingly playing the trick like good sports with nothing important left to lose but their money. There were some blue-collar types—dirty whites and cleaned-up Mexicans—out on a roll, spending gaudily as only true paupers do on an occasion. There were also some rich men's sons, out from the fraternity house, interested in learning about life and willing to spend a fortune to do so. The men, one and all, were piqued to discomfort by the nonstop barrage of sexual stimuli. Far beyond arousal, they were at the point of drunken torpor. The room was stuffy and pregnant with charged air, like that near a bullfight, and it seemed a gang rape could ensue at the wrong word from the emcee. He was a bleak and desperate comedian type, hiding beneath layers of fat, a leather biker jacket, and the pretend glory of working with so many beautiful women. He seemed to know this secret word with which to set off the crowd, but for the moment was unwilling to utter it.

Despite the copious security—huge, round men in black windbreakers who really seemed ready to join in any mass violence, only the stupidest of them radiating any loyalty from their blankish stares—the atmosphere was corrosive. Leering, cheering, *paying* customers, including Kathleen Sanger, called for more. Jumper was on his knees at the edge of the wrestling ring, a red squeeze bottle, originally designed to dispense ketchup but now filled with oil, in his hand. He was in the process of dribbling said oil into the pressed-together bosom of a bikini rhinestone cowgirl. Suddenly striding into the midst of the sex palace and our group, walking right up and hideously halting right in front of Jumper's face, was the overbearing presence of Naomi Sussman. Made even more unattractive in comparison to the young working women, she wielded her unpleasantness like a blunt instrument.

"I just got word your mother died," she crowed at Jumper. "Don't bother coming home tonight, you son of a bitch." Oil oozed guiltily from the neck of the bottle clutched in Jumper's hand and spread in a creeping pattern up his shirt cuff. His wife marched away like a hunchback, dragging her festering wake of misery behind her.

Jumper, incredibly, put down his oil, sat back in his chair

next to his bemused shaman, and reapplied a match to his resting cigar. "Jesus, Jackie must have told her I was here," was all he said. I knew I had seen into the true heart of their marriage, and where some feeling should have reigned, there was only an inhuman abyss.

One woman, dressed like a Civil War soldier in a thong bathing suit bottom, crushed her breasts around the young comic actor Adragna's head. Her partner, costumed as a fire-fighter with hardly anything on under her flameproof coat, did the same to me, breathing into my ear, "I've written a screen-play, and I'd do anything to have you take a look at it."

Overloaded by sensation, beside himself with lust, horror, and heavy conscience, Adragna mumbled, "This place . . . is everything wrong with our world . . ."

"Oh, no, my friend," I replied. "This isn't the half of it." Jumper had just completed a several-hundred-dollar bid that had Bell in a dressing room changing into shorts and then entering the mud ring when I fled the scene without saying good-bye to anyone.

Returning home for the first time in a week, I flung myself through the door. I crossed the room and tore the answering machine, its steady, unblinking light glowing a ferocious red, out of the wall. It was just a reminder of the relentless dis-connection of life here. I went into the bathroom and turned on the water in both the sink and the tub, hoping to drown out the roaring seashell sound of emptiness inside me. I sat down limply on the toilet. I could hear the rushing water, feel the cool porcelain around me, smell the anise scent of ab-sinthe all over. Sliding onto the floor in a heap, I felt a wave of exhaustion come over me, an exhaustion one, or even several, nights of good sleep could not erase. It surrounded my spine like a bath of ice and paralyzed me. I hit the light switch and was enveloped in blackness; it was either that or shave my eyeballs with a razor.

CHAPTER TEN

The next day was a ridiculously hot and bright one even by Wormwood standards. I dragged myself through a blistering sun into the office where I received the last work I would read and comment on—the novel by Weissbrot. At twenty-three, two years into my tenure out here, I felt like the youngest case of burnout on the books. I had heard and seen and smelled my fill of this fetid place, and was ready to disengage from it. I would have tossed aside my work altogether if not for the particular piece I signed for from the foggy haze behind my desk.

"Weissbrot," I said to myself as I wrote up my facile summary and critique, "I've come to the end here, good fellow. Until I figure out where to go next, I'll just be going through the motions, trying to hang on, but for you I'll do this. I'll read this last one carefully, and give you one more from the guts. They say that 'wormwood voideth away the worms of the guts,' ol' Weissbrot, but I've got a bit left of each, so I'll do this for you." I felt close to the absent author, as if we had mysteriously become friends. I figured he would have given it to me straight and shot from the hip if our roles were reversed. He was not one of those simpering, well-meaning script writers I'd read so much, who tried to please audience and critic alike with every false, feel-good thought and word. No, he was a hard-slugging novelist who told it the way it was, in all its ugly splendor, and he must have known where this would leave him. I worked through the night, writing the honest coverage that would doom his work to obscurity, and then I drank until my absinthe was done. I took a phone call from Jumper Sussman, who wanted the goods and showed no sign of remorse, no disruption in schedule over his mother's death, and then I went out to the reflecting pool to watch the sun crawl up into the sky.

Out at the pool's edge I felt like a condemned man. The hours until my final moment were ticking away, and rather than any ephiphany of great clarity, I could only focus on the time slipping through my fingers and my lack of epiphanies. For a moment I considered a last memo I could write to spark a bit of a blaze of glory in which to go out—an obituary placed in the trades for Sussman's mother. I could write it up on studio letterhead, suggesting donations to Jumper in lieu of flowers, and a memorial service to be held at the Mons Veneris mudwrestleteria. My amusement quickly left me, though, as I realized the pointlessness of the gesture. It was a sure sign of my years here that I would even consider such a small, cruel act. No, what I needed to do was something positive, an act that would benefit a deserving person. I thought of the coverage resting in my fax machine, splashed through my rippling reflection in the black water, and started back toward The Bunker.

Sitting down at my desk, I ripped the pages I had previously written out of the fax machine and stuffed them into my pocket. I checked my watch and saw I had only forty minutes left before a staff meeting that would be the last convincing moment I could deliver my new coverage. I called up a fresh document on my computer screen and began typing with abandon. "To call *No Rewards for the Deserving*, by Weissbrot, well written is to use extreme restraint," I began. "Was *Moby Dick* just another fish story?" Perhaps the *Moby Dick* stuff was a little much, but nothing succeeded like excess in this place. "More important," I continued, "this book packs the double threat of being a work of literature that also *begs* to be brought to screen. With humor that scales the heights of *Sillyman*"—I invoked the name of a blockbuster comedy that had grossed near $200 million—"and pathos along the lines of *Sutton— A Life*"—I referenced the touching past summer hit that earned Alan Asher his Oscar and put $150 million domestic into a rival studio's coffers. I paused for a moment, wasting valuable time, while I tried to conjure a third mega-successful film that would irresistibly bait the hook for Jumper and Sanger. I considered some classic animated features which I could analogize, but decided it was just too far a stretch. Finally it occurred to me. "It has the feeling of *Summer Stock and Barnstormers*, without songs," I wrote of the musical that held a special place in American film history. "And beyond all this,"

I promised, "this book is new, and fresh, and unlike *anything* we've ever seen before." It was a leap, but the grasping, lemming-like, fear-ridden, drugged-up, deluded bastards just might go for it.

I feverishly outlined a filmic plot that the novel didn't really possess. I tried to give the work a mystique of quality and commerciality, and to imply the need to move with alacrity before other studios got involved. "If I only had more time," I lamented to myself as I printed my new coverage with all the X's in the excellent column. I wrote that copies of the book would follow shortly and then locked the manuscript in my bottom desk drawer amongst my absinthe paraphenalia. I faxed a copy to Jumper's office and cc'd Kathleen Sanger. My final move was to fax a copy of the glowing coverage to the story editor at another studio under the guise of "I know I shouldn't be doing this, but on the off chance Jumper passes, I feel compelled to help bring this work to screen. . . ."

Sending the faxes away, I felt the tumblers, well oiled by my recent actions—the memo, the lies, the absinthe, my crying out with Ronnie—all start to line up. The lock was about to be turned and the door flung open, and there was nothing I could do to stop it and nothing I could do to find out what was on the other side. It filled me with my own brand of fear. Not insecure, piddling worry about my own welfare, but an edgy, blinding admiration for the awesome fiscal carnage I might have loosed. Along with it there was a cheap but riveting excitement too, for what might be my outcome, and whom I might be after the smoke cleared. I sat back and watched.

At 9:00 A.M. Jumper called to confirm if the book was truly as good as I had written. "You don't know the half of it, boss," I said, and he hurried off the phone.

By 9:05 I dialed Kathleen Sanger. "Hi, Kathleen. I just wanted to let you know that I would *love* to be further involved in the Weissbrot book—"

"Sorry, Nathan," she said, profoundly unsorry and immediately all claws. "No offense, but you're going to have to just move out of our way here. This thing's boiling over, and we don't have time for any hand holding," she barked at me.

At 9:20 Bell stuck his fat face into my office and smiled. "I know I don't usually come down here into the belly of the beast, but I think I'm looking at V.P. stripes over this one. Let's go do some whoring tonight when the deal's closed, Nathan. My treat."

"What can I say, Chick, I'm touched," I responded as he ducked back out of my doorway.

At 10:15 Ben Offerman, head of Business Affairs, called me to inquire into the relative budget range of the project.

"Well, Ben, the thing *can* be pulled off cheaply—say, the forty to fifty million range. . . . But that may be selling it short of it's full filmic potential. Still, though, even with the visual effects and computer graphics, there's no reason this can't be brought in under triple-digit millions."

"Uh-huh," Offerman said as I heard his pen scratching out figures, "that jibes with what Jumper told me." He hung up, leaving me impressed at Jumper's ability to budget a nonexistent movie.

At 11:10 I got word from Jackie that the studio's offer was

being considered, but competition from other studios was fierce.

Wracked with anticipation and incredulity, as if watching a balloon inflate to the point of near explosion, I waited. I pictured Weissbrot, dumbfounded by his good fortune, sitting in some cheap apartment like mine, suddenly faced with the prospect of making more money than he had previously thought possible. I hoped all that money wouldn't be a curse, that I hadn't burdened him with it. I imagined his agent wringing maximum bucks out of the unforeseen situation. I figured the studio would try to wrap it up before lunch or that perhaps they would realize no one amongst them had read the book and I would be terminated with extreme prejudice.

I got the celebratory e-mail at 12:20. . . .

Memorandum
To: *Executive Staff*
From: *Jumper*
Re: *New Acquisition*

Congratulations to Kathleen Sanger, Ben Offerman, and the rest of the Creative Group. After a spirited bidding war, we have secured film rights to No Rewards for the Deserving, by Weissbrot, for 1.7 million dollars against $2.4 million upon production. I am proud to be involved with a work that so embraces the very fabric of American life and portrays it in such a fresh way. I am confident of this material's filmic success. Trade announcements will follow. Preliminary casting to coincide with the adaptation.

Soon after, I received another e-mail from Kathleen Sanger explaining why I would need to be left out of the press release in order to emphasize "the new regime's chain of command," but my role in this would not be forgotten and "where the hell was that copy of the manuscript?" . . . Then, about an hour later, the call came.

"Please report to my office," said Kathleen Sanger, self-appointed inquisitor on the matter of memoranda.

Walking up from my basement hovel, across The Bunker's courtyard, and up to her lair, I felt an acute sense of awareness come over me. I knew where the meeting would head. I knew exactly what I would have to say in order to keep my job. I felt no sense of willingness in me to say those things, though. I stepped through the waiting area outside Kathleen's office, moving right for her door. Her assistant tried to stop me with a verbal protest, but I gave her an intractable look. She knew that I knew she listened to all of her boss's calls, and neither of us was unaware of what the meeting would entail. She left her cubicle for the ladies' room, and I gave her a moment to get away, so Kathleen wouldn't blame her when I breezed in. After the perfunctory beat, however, I did breeze in, and enjoyed doing so.

Kathleen looked up from reading a sheaf of faxed pages. She was mad-eyed, pupils unfocused, and had a ring of garish orange lipstick sloppily framing her mouth. I kicked her door shut, leaving, I noted with great satisfaction, a deep heel scuff on its surface. I threw myself into a chair, draping a leg over its arm, and smiled at her. This woman, despite the scripts

on her desk, and movie posters on her walls, had gotten into
the business for this very occasion. She lived to get a fast grip
on a rival's balls, to drop the ax. Now, today, she would have
had mine, except I hadn't needed a real set since I'd been in
the industry, and felt like I'd left them at home safely in my
other suit.

"What can I do for you?" I asked, hoping my nonchalant
tone would deprive her of the satisfaction of crushing me in
her cool fist.

"What the hell is this?" she asked, waving several pages
of Weissbrot's manuscript at me. I supposed she'd had it sent
over from Weissbrot's happy and newly wealthy agent.

"That is a very expensive pile of paper," I said. She
clenched her jaw, and the skin of her heavily made-up face
undulated in contained fury.

"There's no movie here," she said, and rattled the pages at
me. "It's nothing like your coverage—"

"It's good to know some of you have read *that* at least."

"I told Jumper you're the one who wrote this memo," she
said directly, holding up another sheet of paper. Apparently
she was unwilling to draw it out if I was unwilling to cower a
little.

"But you can't know that for sure," I said, and shrugged.
My mind was blank.

"I know you're behind that mock Terry Mauve script too,"
she said, her eyelids fluttering. It seemed she was forcing her
eyes to bore into me, fighting to keep them from wandering.
She must've gotten ahold of whatever the Sussmans had been
taking, for she too had their glazed effect. "And now the final

touch with this coverage . . . the studio is giving you a chance to quit. I wouldn't."

"Then what can I say but congratulations on your new acquisition?" I smiled again, causing her to sling a bowl of hard candies at me.

We entered Jumper's master suite in the executive offices moments later to find him pedaling away on his Exercycle, an unlit cigar in his mouth. He wore a sweatsuit, had an immaculate white towel tucked around his neck, and was huffing and puffing into a speaker phone. Naomi sat off to the side, drilling Jackie on some unsavory task as Kathleen marched me in, the cavalier delivering a prisoner to her king. This was her moment. She had taken on the assignment of discovering who was behind the satirical subterfuge and pure treason, and she had succeeded. She had gone outside normal work tasks and gotten the job done, and it would establish her as a henchman to be reckoned with in town.

"Nathan," Jumper said as evenly as he could from his bike.

"Jumper," I answered.

"Good work on the Weissbrot book," he began.

"Well, my heart was in it," I said. I took my original coverage from my pocket and handed it to Jumper. "You'll probably be wanting this." His pedaling slowed to a near stop as he skimmed over my words. He looked up and cast a searching look at Sanger. Her bitter nod confirmed things, and Sussman's face slowly marbelized in front of my eyes. Lines and fissures I had never recognized before suddenly ran deep and severe.

"This too . . . Well, you cost me a lot of money this morning," he said, an undertone of anger creeping into his voice.

"The studio's, not yours," I corrected.

"One and the same. Has anything else come in since?" he asked, slowly moving into position.

"Not across my desk," I mustered truthfully. For a moment there was only the whooshing sound of the cycle's fly wheel rotating mechanically.

"Are you still feeling challenged where you are? Maybe you'd like to try something in marketing?" Jumper offered, proceeding technically, working his cycle's pedals methodically now.

"If I were to stay at this job, it would have to be with the understanding that I could speak my mind," I said, pushing ahead.

"What's that supposed to mean?" Naomi screeched, breaking the form of the entire encounter in her bullish, miserable way. Jumper cringed and slowed down his ride. Only Kathleen smiled at her benignly.

"It means I should be free to say when I think a project is worthless. Like yours, for instance. What an unrelenting piece of garbage," I said deliberately. The comment seemed to take the oxygen right out of the room. Jackie, sitting on the couch, looked both thrilled and melancholy.

"I'm leaving for Europe," Naomi said. "I'm sure I won't be seeing you when I get back." She got up and walked out, the office vibrating from all the wretchedness and unattractiveness she left behind her like a slug's trail.

"One thing you should know, Nathan, is that you didn't

really do any damage. It doesn't matter what the project is. As long as we're the ones who get it, then the perception is that we're the winners," Jumper stated. I nodded robotically. Of course, I knew he was right, and I also knew that I would never know all that he did about this game.

"I'm resigning to pursue other opportunities," I said as evenly as I could, finally stating what everyone in the room, including myself, wanted to hear. Although this time I had spoken my own destiny, the moment lacked the showiness of my firing from the agency, possibly because Jumper, Kathleen, the departed Naomi, and maybe Jackie as well were logy from their medications. Their reactions meant nothing to me, but if only I could have wiped the look of victory off Sanger's face.

"Listen, Nathan," Jumper said, "just because you're not going to be working here doesn't mean we can't stay in touch. If there's anything we can do for you . . ." he continued, ridiculous in his insincerity as he sat there, cigar hanging dormant, like an ornament, from his sweaty, purple lips. He couldn't even smoke with conviction. "Or if there's anything you want to bring in to us . . ." he went on.

Ah, there it is, I thought, the insurance clause in case I might present a project of value to them in the future. But I wouldn't. I could now admit to myself the truth I had denied for so long—that I had nothing to say. I didn't have some secret, profound story lodged in me, burning to come out and be shown on the big screen. "Naturally you won't be given severance and your pension plan contributions will be revoked. . . ." Jumper added. I began walking out, and as I left the office, the last thing I saw was Jumper pedaling up to full

speed again, dabbing himself with that white towel, and raising a fist to me as a strange sign of goodwill or solidarity.
Behind me I faintly heard Kathleen ask, "Should I take him
off the Rolodex?"

It was evening, and once again time for a job-ending
bender; only this time there was no doubt as to what would
be my drink. I killed the dregs of my absinthe and tossed the
bottle into the garbage along with my studio identification and
office key. Holding my copy of Weissbrot's manuscript as a
totem, I walked to my car and drove off the lot. I handed in
my parking pass at the gate and left a note for the night guard,
instructing him on how to get his script to Jared for consideration.

I steered my car out the studio gates and onto the nearby
surface streets. Menace came up in waves off the baking
roads. I looked into the distance at the snowy mountain peaks
which seemed to call out to me—a sound that was faint yet
cautionary. I now understood it was the low roar of evil psalms
reverberating from the studio, and that they could be heard
all over this town. They could be heard in the buzzing of the
high-voltage lines that draped over all the buildings and radiated from the deluge of neon along the roadsides here. They
could be felt when the earth rumbled and shook. They could
be seen shining on screens across the city and beyond. All
but ready to point myself past those mountains, one thing held
me back—tonight there was a charity gala for the Children's
Hospital that would grant me one more chance to see Ronnie.
I could not force myself to pass it up. So I turned around and

headed not toward the distant, solemn mountains, but rather over the nearby parched rolling hills into the sea of gleaming, seething lights amongst which the town's people tried to hide.

That night I pulled into the mass of fine cars at the luxurious citadel home which was the location of my last industry function. I breathed deeply, pulling myself together to face the wolves who were always out after one had left a job under questionable circumstances. Overworked valets tended to abandoned vehicles, and I vaguely remembered another affair I had been to at this same house. For a moment I wasn't sure of the occasion, only that it had been during the day, and had to do with pink flamingoes. I was then struck by the odd attire of some, then all, of the guests who flowed into the house. They wore various forms of underwear—silk and mesh with elaborate underwires on the women, jockey-like colors on the shorts of the men. I remembered that this was a theme party, and the theme for the evening was lingerie.

Trying to move through the door in a subtle fashion, I was halted by two competent-looking, codpiece-wearing doormen. They quickly convinced me that entering the party fully clothed was not a possibility, and I felt my dismay rise as I saw frighteningly handsome women walk in around me wearing lacy undergarments as if straight off catwalks or the pages of fashion magazines. Buttery-skinned, prosperous-looking men were clad in dinner jackets and bowties with no shirts, and modestly cut, shiny, and richly patterned boxer shorts. I was miserable as I kicked off my shoes and pulled down my pants in the foyer, finally feeling that I had reason to wear the sexy pair of underwear Ronnie had given me as a gift so many weeks ago. Of course, I wasn't wearing them. I never had. Instead I had slept many nights with them clenched in my hands, as some kind of superstitious link to her.

Tonight, though, my underwear was a shameful pair of skivvies that had been worn too many times since their last washing. The dingy briefs were one of the few pairs I still possessed after suffering the laundry room burglary. They gaped around my depleted legs and gaunt waist. Now, here I was in an uninteresting sports coat, sorry loafers, and embarrassing drawers, amongst the most image-conscious people in the world. I immediately went for the bar and found the host was well prepared with a deep supply of my now trendy green beauty.

Before long, I was nose deep and quickly forgetting what I could of the finality of the day, but I was in the wrong place to forget. Walking along the length of the pool, full of lily pads and rubber floating frogs, I stumbled into Feller. He had seemingly grown taller and had become physically fit since I'd last seen him. His abdomen was cut into geometric quadrants, and his previously wiry hair was now straightened and slicked back. Even the bags under his eyes had grown invisible due to a deep suntan. He stood with Patrick Hackman, whom he now represented.

"We took that project you guys unloaded into turnaround," Feller said to me as I drew near. "We set it up over at Eddie Upland's company."

"What project's that?" I wondered. Feller looked at me blankly for a moment, then waved at Upland, who stood across the pool wearing a long nightshirt. Upland was speaking to a notoriously womanizing martial arts star who stood proudly in a pair of leopard print slingshot bikini briefs. The two of them appeared to be embroiled in the manly sharing of tales of female conquest, replete with hand gestures. Breaking away upon Feller's wave, Upland began waltzing over toward us. In the course of his trip of a few feet it seemed as if the nightshirt became a caftan as he assumed a precious and feminine air, created especially for Feller, I imagined.

Snatching a bite-sized piece of duck sausage and goat cheese pizza from a passing waiter, Upland intoned loudly, "I heard there's a big opening in the Story Department at a certain studio . . ." before sashaying on again.

Feller looked at me like a piece of carrion, and seemed to suddenly have business with someone else across the pool. Hackman was on his way as well, but took time to pontificate.

"Kid," he said, "you can always count on getting fired in this town. That's why I became a writer."

"I quit."

"Sure, kid, but you can count on getting fired. So if you write, then at least if you get fired, you've still got that."

"But you're no writer, you're just a goddamned dabbler, Patrick." I smiled.

"Prick," he retorted, and hurried off after his agent.

Blissfully alone in the crowd and already drunk, I looked for Ronnie. She was the sole reason I remained. I surveyed the now boiling lingerie party in front of me. Sex games had begun in the pool amongst the lily pads, and there was the Children's Hospital mock fund-raising thermometer off to the side, the red line nearly at its goal. A slave sale began, an auctioneer barking into a microphone as the martial arts star in his leopard g-string paraded on an elevated block.

"Come on, ladies—gentlemen too—who'll push the bid into five figures for an evening with this fantastic specimen in front of us. Think of those sick little kids . . . and don't worry, we won't ask if you won't tell what goes on between you," the barker said. He continued promising how much good the proceeds would do, and hands were raised, wildly upping the bid. I saw Feller's hand go up several times until the bidding did reach five figures and he bitterly dropped out.

Suddenly there was a stir across the pool area, and I knew it could be her. Unfortunately, like a recurring nightmare, Kathleen Sanger, dressed in black patent leather bra and panties, stepped through the glass door onto the patio and into my view. She looked like a Roman gladiator. The sight of her caused me to toss back what was left of my drink and signal for another when suddenly, next to Kathleen, *she* appeared. Ronnie, her hair flying in the tropical breeze, stepped outside in florid emerald silks, covered only fleetingly by a black cape. I raised a feeble wave to her, but just as I did she turned away. Instead Kathleen waved back. I brought my hand down and looked at them there, framed in the window, a velvety blur of color, as if painted by Degas. They nodded casually this way and that to admirers from the business who paid the two of them great attention. Kathleen's arm slid intimately around Ronnie's waist beneath her cape, and my lady of oblivion leaned into my past tormentor with more tenderness than she'd ever shown me. I nodded, understanding everything—

the timing of our meeting, the cryptic locations, what I now knew as Kathleen's car parked in front of her house. The distance between Ronnie and I swam before my eyes. I took one step and then another around the edge of the pool and toward her.

By the time I reached the patio Chick Bell was standing beside Ronnie, kissing her twice on each cheek, as had become the fashion. He wore ruggedly soled boots, and his tanned belly hung tautly over polka-dotted undershorts. As I came into range, Ronnie's expression grew far away, unknowing of me, while Bell's grew dark and angry.

"You son of a bitch," he snarled at me. "The Weissbrot book'll cost me six more months at director of development." He seemed half ready to fight me.

"It had nothing to do with you," I said.

"Don't mind him," Ronnie said of me. "I have a feeling you'll be moving up the ladder sooner than that." She took Chick by the elbow to lead him into the house. Before she could, I held her by the shoulder.

"What is it?" she asked testily as Chick impatiently pawed at the carpet a few feet ahead of her.

"I've been trying to find you for so long," I blurted. She appraised me coolly, and after a second's delay I heard my own words ring thickly in my ears like a slowed recording. I sounded desperate and realized I was intoxicated again, under the influence of wormwood.

"I wanted you to. I wanted it to be hard." She smiled her beautiful, vicious smile.

I wished to ask her if it had all been for Kathleen and her

job, to tell her I didn't care anyway, but the words stuck in my throat. She looked through me, finished with me for good. She turned and disappeared into the fleshy crowd. I took a step after her, fumbling for her cape, when the heel of Chick's hand found the bridge of my nose with force. I spun to the ground, dark images of the party around me forming a swirling collage.

When I became able, I sat, then stood, and floundered after them. I crossed through the living room and ventured deeper into the house. I wandered down hall after hall, past glossy pieces of Empire furniture, past the caterer's setups, and waiters taking breaks, and finally up into the bedroom wing, looking in each part of the giant house for Ronnie. I do not know how long I looked before I reached a locked door and, shaking the knob, heard her voice clearly: "You're in rare company . . ." I heard her say through the door, and then I recognized the distinctive giggle of my former colleague, Chick Bell. I jerked myself away from the door as if it were on fire.

Coming back down the stairs, I made to leave for good, when I saw Shelby Stark standing at the base of the staircase. She stood disconsolate in a somber camisole. Loose, grimy beige stockings hung slackly from her skeletal legs and were gathered up by stringy garters. Moving closer, I saw that her hair was limp and oily, her complexion ashen, and her eyes dead. I remembered all the pretty green bottles lining the shelves in her dining room, and realized that they were absinthe flagons. Empty. She, just as I, just as all of them would sooner or later become, was ensnared, like a small animal caught in the hyacinths and drowning in a swamp. She moved next to me and took my hand. She entwined her clammy, sucking fingers in mine, tugging me up and away from the rest of the party, leading me to an unoccupied, unfurnished room in the house where I finally succumbed.

There was a cavelike darkness to the room, and her tongue flipped about mine desolately. Her skin tasted salty and acrid, but I did not pull away. There was no way I was going to stop now, for I was a machine that had been programmed long ago, still only able to perform a single function although it had long ago become obsolete. Tangled on the floor, we struggled, gaining and losing feeling as we lost and gained clarity. I had become just another of those who were completely divided. My cock and myself were two separate entities. Shelby's pelvic architecture was a yielding, pulsing abyss. While Ronnie had been fiery and full of life, yet somehow unrelenting, unforgiving, and greedy, Shelby was dry, wilted, and vacant. Nonetheless I found myself fucking away, stabbing in the dark, plunging wildly with no hope of reaching the core. I rose above her, my hot semen burning across her skin. Tears came to my eyes and fell. Even during the briefest moment of climax, while vaguely orbiting the lost place inside me that held my secret answers, I could only draw close enough to make out a flaming corona of madness before it was all over and I collapsed off to the side of her.

A moment later she stirred. "You call out when you come," Shelby informed me.

"What did I say?"

"Ronnie. You said Ronnie. Sylvan, I imagine, the way you chase her around," and with that she scurried toward the door, seeming to disappear altogether at the threshold. A moment later a closet door across the room slid open, and someone else, the outline of a strange optical apparatus visible on his head, hurried out after her. Her husband, Don, I figured, finally having gotten his chance to watch through night-vision goggles.

I rolled away, shielding my eyes, against what I did not know in the empty and darkened room. I was somehow stranded one moment behind myself, stuck living one step behind the present. I was supposed to have succeeded here, to have risen to the top, made friends, won influence, married, had a family, donated to charities, become a community leader, returned home a hero. But I could not even understand all those things now. Instead I needed only to get away from the canyon calls from cellular phones, the earthquakes, the studios, the expensive habits, the stripper-screenwriters and actor-whores. I was tired of going to work, talking the phony talk, reading the lousy scripts, whacking the brush for hot tips, paying tribute. I lacked the ability to praise unworthy stories and their creators, and it had cost me dearly. I was exhausted, spent, through with opening my eyes, putting my ear to the ground; my lungs were sick of breathing, my heart tired of beating.

I slunk down the stairs and crossed the living room toward the door. I got one last look at the pool area through the bay window. There was a writhing but mechanical, orgiastic nature to the scene out there that could have been so good, so healing, had it all actually been about charity, or connection, or even fulfillment rather than the simple feeding of fear. The fear of growing old, of fading away, of not meaning anything. Everybody was so pretty, so fragile and desperate, that the image of prowling dogs looking to mount one weaker came back to me. But upon seeing them all unclothed, I realized the image no longer fit. We were not ranging dogs, but hairless baby rodents, huddled together and shaking, our sealed eyes not yet fit for light.

I left that mansion and all the rest behind me, and upon arrival at the cracker box, the isolation settled immediately, formless and screaming. That night as I slept, gone were the graphic dreams of the past in which I was a victim boiled by cannibals or dismembered internally by an assailant. What took their place were dark, empty spaces that neither offered diversion nor woke me up, but instead filled my sleeping mind with quiet, undeniable dread. My old dreams were friendly in comparison to the blackness. When I rose, it might have been days later. The looming spaces remained, but were less dreadful, and I hoped they would become less so with each passing day. I knew now that the wheel had gone around again, and it was time to move on and find what life held for me next, what it might offer instead of the lies, the false laughter, the bunch of laughing images that I had found so far. Finally, after several days had elapsed, I was unsure how many, I emerged from the cracker box as if it were a chrysalis, and was aware my life there would now consist only of putting my belongings in boxes.

Acknowledgments:

I wish to thank my editor Susan Dalsimer, for standing by me and for greatly improving this book. My thanks to Seth Jaret and Dan Mandel for their confidence and belief.

I am grateful to Harvey Weinstein and Bob Weinstein, the rarest of beings in their business, individuals who possess their own opinion.

Great thanks also to Brian Koppelman for lifelong support and for being my first reader.